PRAISE FOR
THE BLOOD GUARD:

"Roy's first novel is the humorous and exciting start of a new trilogy. . . .
The stakes are raised with a startling revelation that will have
readers eager for the next book."
—*Kirkus Reviews*

"Breathless action, witty dialogue, and unabashed fun."
—*Publishers Weekly*

"[H]its the ground running and doesn't let up until the end."
—*Booklist*

"[A] superbly written adventure . . . has just the right amount of sarcastic
humor and genuine heart . . . a great start to what is sure to be a wildly
popular series . . . a must-have."
—*VOYA*, Highlighted Review

"Intense, action-filled. . . *The Blood Guard* is a non-put-downable page-turner. . . .
This book is a must-have."
—*The Guardian.com*

"Very fun. . . . Surprisingly chilling. . . .
The whole book caught me by surprise."
—*Pixelated Geek*

"This is an action-packed book you never want to put down."
—*Denver Post*

"Wildly intense and deviously funny, *The Blood Guard* has real heart as well
as characters you'll fall in love with. This is cool stuff, very cool stuff."
—MICHAEL GRANT, *New York Times* bestselling author of the Gone series

THE GLASS GAUNTLET

Also by Carter Roy

THE BLOOD GUARD

THE BLOOD GUARD BOOK 2

THE GLASS GAUNTLET

CARTER ROY

two lions

Text copyright © 2015 by The Inkhouse

Published by Two Lions, New York

www.apub.com

Amazon, the Amazon logo, and Two Lions are trademarks of Amazon.com, Inc., or its affiliates.

ISBN 978-1-4778-2626-3 (hardcover)
ISBN 978-1-4778-2715-4 (paperback)
ISBN 978-1-4778-7625-1 (ebook)

Book design by Tanya Ross-Hughes

Printed in the United States of America

First edition

10 9 8 7 6 5 4 3 2 1

Again and always,
for Beth

PROLOGUE
MY DAD IS A BAD GUY

I'm not my father's biggest fan.

Not just because he ordered a flunky to kill me the last time I saw him (which has got to be some kind of new low in bad parenting). And not because of his secret identity as the head of the Bend Sinister, an evil society working to bring about the end of the world. All of that is bad enough, but even worse? He stole a person's soul.

He combed it right out of her body using this strange device called the Eye of the Needle, then escaped before the Blood Guard were able to catch him.

Sometimes I look at my new friend Sammy, and I almost think that because he's an orphan and never knew his dad at all, he's had it easy.

Which is pretty messed up.

At least *I* still have my mom.

"When are we going after dad?" I asked her for the zillionth time while we were loading up a battered old white van.

"Not going to tell you," she replied, as usual. "So stop asking."

My mother is pretty much the exact opposite of my dad. She's one of the good guys.

In addition to being pretty, and scary smart, and the kind of mom other kids wish they had for their own, she is one of a group of elite knights known as the Blood Guard. Thanks to her training, she is handy with all sorts of weapons, but especially the sword—I've seen her deflect bullets with a blade, she is that good. Which is why I listened when she told me, "Ronan, go help Jack."

"Sure thing." I set down a plastic crate of food and went over to the other van, where my friends were tallying things on a clipboard.

"So how are we going to catch my da—" I started to ask Dawkins, but then caught myself; I didn't want this to sound personal. "The Bend Sinister Head?" I smacked my fist into my open palm.

Dawkins raised an eyebrow. "What's that you did there just now?"

"This?" I punched my hand again. "You know, to show I mean business."

"What, like you're going to *hit* him?" Dawkins snorted. "Do you expect him to cower and quake at the fearsome might of *you*—thirteen-year-old Evelyn Truelove?" In his dirty black jeans, T-shirt, and brown leather jacket, Jack Dawkins looks like a late-teens hipster, but he's actually closer to two hundred years old. Like everyone else in my life, he's not exactly what he appears to be. He is something called an Overseer in the Blood Guard, and because of that, he doesn't age and he can't be killed.

But he *can* be hurt. So I slugged him.

I really hate being called Evelyn.

"Wretched boy!" he said, rubbing his bicep. "Tell me, do you happen to know where your dad and the Bend Sinister *are*?"

"Um . . . no," I mumbled.

"Precisely," Dawkins said. "Ergo, we cannot go after him. Once we figure out where he's gone, we will come down on him and his cronies like a rain of clever, dashingly handsome hellfire."

"I don't think hellfire can be handsome," Greta said, pushing her red hair out of her face.

"Or clever," Sammy added.

Dawkins waved away their objections. "My point is that until we find a solid lead, all we can do is lie low and regroup. Or rather, that's what *I* will do. You three are going to be working yourselves silly, learning the art and mysteries of the Blood Guard!"

Which is why we were leaving the Arlington safe house. Not only the three of us, but my mom and Greta's dad; Dawkins and another Overseer named Ogabe; and a half-dozen Blood Guard who'd answered our call for help when we faced off against the Bend Sinister in an underground power plant a week ago.

"I can't wait," I said and meant it. "Is this place we're going some kind of high-tech training center?"

"Not . . . exactly," Dawkins said, keeping his eyes on his clipboard.

Sammy smiled. "Are there, like, target ranges, and dueling robots with laser beams, and—"

"Robots? Laser beams?" Dawkins laughed. "Does the Blood Guard look like the CIA to you? Do you think the government funds us? No. Ours is a very low-cost operation."

"You guys at least have a school, right?" Greta asked.

"What confuses you about the words *low* and *cost*?"

"There's not even a school?" Greta frowned.

"It's summer!" Dawkins said. "Why would you want to be packed off to a lousy school? Bor-ing! Instead, imagine this: A mountain retreat! Nature in its . . . natural surroundings!"

"Which is where it's usually found," Greta pointed out.

"But there is a computer center, right?" Sammy was a serious gamer and an even more serious hacker in training.

"*Low-cost* as in *poor*," Dawkins finally said. "*Low-cost* as in we are a secret society, and we can't afford to be noticed . . . nor, sadly, can we afford much of anything at all."

The white vans we were loading *were* pretty beat-up, it was true.

"We've never officially trained any Blood Guard candidates before. You three are the first." Dawkins' face broke out into the enormous smile he uses when he's trying to be charming. "But trust me: You are going to *love* this place!"

CHAPTER 1

HOW I SPENT MY SUMMER VACATION

We hated it.

Greta maybe most of all.

None of us were allowed to leave the moldy old ghost town of Wilson Peak, or to call or email anyone. Greta took that personally. "My mom turns forty on September second," she explained. "No stupid summer camp is going to make me miss her birthday."

"It's just a birthday," Sammy said. "You can be there for her next one."

"No." Greta scowled. "I'm going to be there for *this* one."

When we first arrived in June, I have to admit we thought the town was kind of cool. Exciting, even. A mountaintop hideaway! The Blood Guard's covert headquarters! A top-secret training camp!

That feeling lasted about ten minutes.

There wasn't a whole lot to the place—four stubby little streets like compass points around a dinky park; an old stone lodge that doubled as the Blood Guard's headquarters; an empty fire station; a boarded-up church; and a couple dozen rotting wooden bungalows, most of them roofless, windowless, and doorless. Our home for the summer.

"Wilson Peak was founded in the 1920s as a winter vacation spot," Dawkins explained as he drove us around, "but it was closed after World War II. The one road up the mountain was fenced off, the place-name erased from maps, the town itself lost to the mists of time—forgotten!"

By everyone except the Blood Guard, that is.

A dozen retired Guard secretly reconnected Wilson Peak to the power grid. They fixed up a few of the ruined buildings, added lines for computers, and surrounded the town with an electric fence to stop people from breaking in.

This was where our training took place.

Each day's classes started after breakfast, with a skinny old lady everyone called the McDermott. She taught the history of the Blood Guard—and a lot of regular history on top of that. Second period, Ogabe instructed us in computer programming and hacking—his specialty. It turned out that Sammy was a natural. Third period, Greta's dad, Mr. Sustermann, who is also a member of the Blood Guard, taught us lock picking, but the only one of us who was ever any good was Greta.

"Guys," she said, rolling her eyes, "that's a Master Lock Number Three—the world's easiest to pick." Greta's my friend now, so I sometimes forget about who she was when I first met her: the world's most annoying honor roll student.

"Let's try again," her dad said, looking at Sammy and me and rolling his eyes like his daughter.

Afternoons, an old dude named Griffin zoomed around in a wheelchair and taught fencing.

"*You're* the teacher?" I'd said in our first class. "Kind of an unfair fight."

"Just try me, sonny!" he said.

I grabbed one of the practice sabers and turned toward him.

Before I took two steps, he popped a wheelie and spun, knocking my sword from my hand with one of his footrests. "It *is* unfair—for you!" he said, laughing and rolling away.

Our days ended with Dawkins' strange classes. And those made no sense at all.

Sometimes he had us play dodgeball—three of us against one. Him.

"You must anticipate your opponent," he said, tapping his temple. "What maneuvers percolate in his superior mind? In which direction will he lunge? Know before he knows it himself!"

"That's nonsense!" Greta said, faking a dodge right before throwing herself left—directly into the path of the red rubber ball Dawkins had already hurled her way.

"That *hurt*!" she complained, getting up.

"Serves you right," Dawkins replied. "That sloppy feint fooled no one."

Another time, he had us fight him on a floor he'd built out of giant ice blocks. It was a square twenty feet wide, the surface ripply and clear, like a boxing ring made of wet glass. Piled at one end were tin cans, sticks of firewood, old shoes, a couple of frying pans, and more lumpy things I couldn't make out.

"My arsenal," he explained, gesturing. "Yours is there." Three swords lay on the ice at the other end. "Can you defend yourselves while coping with a difficult environment? Can you keep your balance while pelted with junk and insults? We shall see." He stood carefully on the ice. "Come and tap me with the point of your blade if you can."

None of us ever got close.

At one point, he hurtled something small and white at me, and instinctively, I swung my blade like a bat.

With a loud *bong!* the object arced high into the air. At the same moment, my feet shot out from under me and my butt slammed down on the ice.

"Disqualified!" Dawkins hollered.

I watched the white dot disappear over the nearest row of bungalows.

"Was that my Mets baseball?" I asked.

"Maybe?" Dawkins squinted after it. "I might have found it on the porch of your cabin."

"That was a collectible!" I protested. "It's valuable."
What I didn't say was *My dad gave it to me.*

"No point crying over lost memorabilia, Ronan." He
reached down and gave me a hand up. "If you must weep,
do so over yet another season the Mets have thrown away."

Our classes with Dawkins were all like that, each
weirder than the last. On the first hot day, he had us use
slingshots to strike a target he'd rigged over the town's
pool. A direct hit would drop him into the water.

He taunted us from his perch. "That the best you got,
Evelyn?"

I couldn't figure out the slingshot's aim, and neither
could Greta. Sammy, though, just stepped up and said,
"You better hold your breath." He closed one eye, drew
back the rubber sling, and let fly.

"And *you* better hold your tongue when speaking—"

The stone *tocked* right into the target's center.

Dawkins plopped into the pool before he could finish
his sentence.

"What is it we're supposed to be learning here?" Greta
asked one day, after a game of Capture the Flag in which
the flag was tied to Dawkins, who ran all over the compound shouting "*Hoo! Hoo!*"

"Everything and nothing. It takes a crazy quilt-work of
skills to become one of the Blood Guard," he explained.
"It may not seem so to you, but that's what you're picking
up here—oddball skills, pieces of the quilt. It's up to you
to stitch them together into a useful whole."

❖ ❖ ❖

Greta's first escape attempt came the second week of July.

She disappeared into the woods with a shovel, and came back that evening, slung over Ogabe's enormous shoulder like a bag of laundry.

"Found her by the south fence." He gently set her on her feet. "Trying to dig her way out."

We had all gathered in the gazebo in the little park at the center of town: Greta's dad; Sammy; me and my mom; and Dawkins and Bentley, a dark gray, floppy-eared Weimaraner puppy who followed Dawkins around like his own personal shadow.

Greta looked like she'd been buried alive—she had dirt caked on her hands and clothes, in her hair, smeared all over her sweaty face. "What's the big deal?" she asked. "I was just digging a hole!"

"You can't go home, Greta," Mr. Sustermann said. "That was the deal. We train you to join the Blood Guard, and you leave your old life behind."

"I never agreed to leave *Mom* behind," Greta said. "Her birthday is coming up."

"I know that," Mr. Sustermann said. "And I also know this is about more than her birthday." He shares his red hair with Greta, but not much else: she's slender and small, and he's big and muscly. "But no matter the real reason, until we locate the Bend Sinister, the safest place for you is here. They could very well be lying in wait for you at your mom's."

"It's Ronan they want, not me," Greta said.

My mom glanced sharply my way. Dad *had* been chasing me, it was true, but that was over. I'd made it clear I wasn't going to join him.

"I need you to promise you won't try this sort of thing again," Dawkins said.

Greta crossed her arms. "Fine. I promise I won't try this sort of thing again." She sniffed her clothes. "If it's okay, I'm going to go and shower. I'm filthy." She walked away toward the bungalow she shared with her dad.

"I'll talk to Greta," Mr. Sustermann said, turning and jogging after her.

"Do you believe that promise?" my mom asked, once they were out of earshot.

"Absolutely not," Dawkins said.

"She gave her word," I protested.

"And I'm sure she will follow her promise to the letter— she won't try digging under the fence again. Instead, it'll be something else."

"She really wants to be home for her mom's birthday," I said.

Dawkins winced. "That's what she says."

"That, and she really hates this place," Sammy said to Ogabe.

Ogabe pointed a finger at us and asked, "And you two? Do you also hate this place?"

"We don't . . . love it," I said.

"Though I do love your coding class," Sammy said.

"Then I take it you finished that program I assigned?"

"Ages ago." Sammy pretended to yawn. "Total piece of cake."

"Let's take a look," Ogabe said. He nodded at us, and then the two of them headed to the lodge.

Dawkins watched them walk off. "I can't watch over Greta all day everyday, Ronan. So it has to be you."

"Me? Spy on her?" I asked. "I can't rat Greta out."

"I'm not asking you to tattle," Dawkins said. "Just . . . if Greta tries to run away, tag along. Make sure to bring the dog." He bent down to Bentley's head and murmured something in her ear. Bentley's tail knocked against my shin. "Slow Greta down until the rest of us can stop her."

"This is what you signed on for, Ronan," my mom said. "You know how important Greta is."

I knew. But Greta? She had no idea.

According to Blood Guard lore, there are thirty-six "Pure" souls in the world—blessed people who are so deep-down *good* that they make up for the nastiness of everybody else. According to Dawkins, if something were to happen to even one of the Pure, the earth would be in danger of ending.

That's where the Blood Guard—and me, if I'm ever allowed to join—come in. We're supposed to protect the Pure—from themselves, and from those who would do them harm.

From people like my dad.

We don't always succeed.

That woman whose soul my dad had stolen and left in a coma? She's one of the Pure. (Her name is Flavia and she's a mom with two little kids, but I guess my dad didn't care about any of that.)

Greta, it turns out, is another Pure. I didn't even want to think what my dad would do to her if he ever found out.

I turned toward Dawkins. "You can count on me."

"Ronan," Dawkins said and clapped me on the back. "Don't you think I knew that already?"

So a week later, when Greta tried to sneak off again, Sammy and I went with her.

"This is my problem, guys," she said.

"Then it's our problem, too," I told her. "We're in this together, right?"

Sammy nodded. "So how are we busting out?"

That time, we were going to tube along a stream down the back of the mountain—right until it disappeared through a metal grate. The time after that, Greta concocted a complicated plan involving crossbows, tree-climbing, and zip-lining over the electrified fence, but even she admitted it was too crazy to attempt. The next week, Greta swiped the spare keys to one of the white vans and, late at night, snuck us into the back before the weekly grocery run. But Bentley sniffed us out, and when the doors opened just before dawn, standing outside were Mr. Sustermann, Dawkins, and my mom.

"Traitor," Greta said to the puppy, scowling.

Bentley hopped into the rear of the van and licked her face.

"Kisses don't make up for betrayal!" she said, but she was laughing.

Dawkins caught my eye and tilted his head toward the dog.

After that, I kept Bentley close.

Early on the first morning of our eleventh week there, Greta woke us up. The sun was barely over the horizon.

"This time, my plan is totally going to work," she announced. "I promise."

Sammy and I went along without asking for details, because that's what friends do.

Which is how the three of us ended up in a line on the crest of a hill on the edge of town. We each sat on a big flattened cardboard box, our legs hooked over the lip of the slope.

"You want to sled down *that*?" Sammy asked, thumping the cardboard. "On *this*?"

I admit: I was nervous, too. The hill was so steep that it felt like I was standing on the edge of a tall building. Below us, the old ski run zigzagged between the trees all the way down the mountain. In winter it would be covered in nice, soft snow, but now, in August, it was overgrown with long yellow grass. It was almost pretty.

But not so pretty that I wanted to go zooming down it on a flimsy sheet of cardboard.

"Are you sure this is a good idea?" I asked.

"Of course I'm sure!" Greta snapped. "People used to go down this thing all the time on skis; we're on boxes, on grass. We'll go tons slower. It's probably safe."

"*Probably*?" Sammy repeated.

"Wait," I said, glancing around. "Where'd Bentley go?"

"The dog?" Greta asked. "Who cares? This is our chance, guys. Before everyone wakes up." She shoved herself forward.

And just like that, she was over the edge.

Gone.

A heartbeat later, a gray blur barreled between me and Sammy.

Greta was rocketing down the hillside—already twenty feet away and gaining speed, but the Weimaraner puppy was a lot faster.

Bentley flung herself into the air, landed on Greta's shoulders, and knocked her forward, off the cardboard and onto the grass. The cardboard bounced over them and kept going.

Greta rolled a few times and came to a stop. "Dumb mutt!" she shouted. "What's wrong with you?"

"My fault, Greta!" called Dawkins, who'd quietly walked up behind us. "I'm afraid when I saw you push off, I sent Bentley to stop you."

The dog wagged her tail, then went over and sat next to Greta.

Greta glared at it.

"Bentley brought you here?" I asked, looking up at Dawkins. The letters YOLO were emblazoned across the chest of his yellow T-shirt. He'd X'd out the final letter with a fat black marker.

"Are you a dog whisperer?" Sammy asked.

We watched Greta stagger up the hill.

"Nah, dogs and I just . . . understand each other. On a level very few can access." Dawkins reached forward and gave Greta a hand up. "I've come with good news. I, Jack Dawkins, am the answer to your prayers!"

"Not *my* prayers," Sammy said.

"Mine neither," Greta said, knocking grass off her jeans.

"You three are tired of Wilson Peak, right?" Dawkins said. "You, Greta, long to escape! You, Ronan, want off of this summer-scorched mountain and back into the game. And you, Samuel . . ."

"I'm pretty happy here, to be honest," Sammy said, shrugging. "I always wanted to go to summer camp."

"So what's this good news?" Greta asked.

"Two things," Dawkins said. "First: you have all been named finalists for an incredibly competitive scholarship. It's called the Glass Gauntlet, and only—"

"*Gauntlet* like *glove*?" I asked.

"More like *test*, or rather, series of tests. As I was saying, only five or six of the cleverest, most daring, most incorrigible orphans are selected."

"We're not orphans," I said.

"*I* am," Sammy said.

"And we are not incorrigible," Greta said.

"So says the career breakout artist," Dawkins said.

"Look, the truth is, I needed a cover story to get onto the grounds where this Glass Gauntlet event is held. I am too old to compete, but you three are perfect. You want to be Blood Guard? Fine. This is your first real mission. You get a fun-filled weekend away, completing tests—"

"How is a weekend full of tests *fun*?" Sammy said.

"Tests can be fun," Greta muttered. "I like tests."

"—while I do a little surreptitious work for the Guard. Everyone gets something they want." He clapped his hands. "But what I want right now is breakfast."

Greta glanced longingly down the hill. Her flattened box was now so far away that it was just a brown dot.

"Sliding on cardboard?" Dawkins asked, ushering us back toward the lodge. "Good idea, but slow. What you want is to be nearly frictionless, right? *My* first stop would have been that ice machine by the storehouse. Those big melting blocks of ice on that endless slope of grass?" He slid one palm over the other. "Would be like riding the nose cone of a rocket."

Greta wasn't listening. "You said you had two pieces of news."

"Ah, yes," Dawkins said. "Ronan's mum has accomplished what none of the rest of us were able to do."

"What's that?" I asked, wondering how long it would be until Greta tried to talk us into riding huge ice cubes down the hill.

"She's found your dad."

CHAPTER 2

THIS IS THE WAY THE WORLD ENDS

I bolted.

Panic squeezed my chest and the next thing I knew I was running. I didn't even know why. I should have been thrilled about my mom finding my dad, right? My father is the ultimate villain—a liar, a killer, a soul-stealer—and I'd been waiting all summer for the Blood Guard to catch him and bring him to justice.

I should have been happy, but I was terrified.

Bentley loped along next to me, having a great time. She probably thought we were just going for a jog.

By the time I reached the gazebo in Wilson Peak's little central park, my sides were burning and my clothes were drenched with sweat. The day was already scorching hot—not exactly sprinting weather.

"Ronan! Stop!"

Greta.

Gasping for breath, she slowed to a walk. "Where are you headed?"

I panted, looking around. "Beats me."

"Well, wherever it is, you're taking me with you." We both leaned over, our hands on our knees, and caught our breath. "Your dad's not going to get you, Ronan. You know that, right?"

Was that it? Was I afraid my dad would "get" me?

Yes. And no. I dreaded facing him again, that was true. He'd tried to *kill* me the last time I saw him. But there was a lot more to it than that. I wasn't a Blood Guard. Yet. I wasn't *anything*. He could come for me, my mom, Sammy, and Greta—destroy everything and everyone I cared about—and I wouldn't be able to stop him. I got lucky the last time we met. I couldn't count on getting lucky again.

"I just don't . . . want to see him." There was no way I could explain to her what I was thinking. The reason my dad was dangerous for Greta was the same reason she couldn't be told about it. Like every Pure, Greta wasn't allowed to *know* she was a Pure.

"You big dope," she said. "You really think they're going to put us in danger again? No way. It will be Ogabe, my dad, and your mom, along with a bunch of the Blood Guard, all of them armed with swords. You and me and Sammy? We'll be off somewhere safe and boring taking a bunch of tests."

I laughed. "Which you, of course, will ace."

"Obviously," she said.

Greta was right. We'd all be safely far away from my dad, and my mom could take care of herself. "Here they come." Down the street, Sammy and Dawkins had just turned the corner. Dawkins waved.

Watching them, Greta said, "I know you and Sammy have been helping Dawkins stop me from escaping."

"No, we haven't!" Bentley's head pivoted back and forth, almost like she was following the conversation. "Okay, maybe a little bit."

"That has to stop. Whether or not the Blood Guard actually catches your dad, I am not coming back to this place." She wouldn't meet my eye. "I know I say it's about my mom's birthday, but it's more than that, Ronan. She had cancer last year. She still needs me. She's back there in Brooklyn, all alone."

"Okay," I said. "But *you* won't be alone. Let me help. After this test thing, we go to Brooklyn to find your mom."

Greta squinted at me. "You promise?"

"Cross my heart and hope—"

"Stop," she said, cutting me off. "No one should hope to die, ever. A promise is enough."

"Then I promise," I said.

"No matter what?" Greta said.

"No matter what."

One wall of the old stone lodge was floor-to-ceiling windows, and there was a fireplace big enough for a person to stand in. It was easy to imagine snow piled high outside those windows and a fire blazing while dozens of skiers sat around sipping mugs of hot chocolate after a freezing day on the slopes. It must have been pretty nice back in the day.

The place looked a lot different now.

The Blood Guard had transformed it into a war room and nerve center, with a half-dozen computers on a huge wooden table that stretched from one end of the room to the other, and as many flat-screen TVs mounted around the fireplace. Whether the dusty chandeliers were turned on or off, the room flickered with a cold electronic light.

Hearing us come in, my mom swiveled her chair around. "Ah, Ronan," she said. "I'm glad Jack tracked you down before we departed."

"Jack said you found Dad," I said.

"We did." She stood. "And because of that, the Blood Guard depart in an hour."

"An hour?" I repeated. "So fast?"

"Our search has lately become more urgent." My mom picked up a remote and cranked up the sound on one of the TVs. "First, because of this."

A news bulletin on one of the networks told the story of some poor guy in Iowa who caught a really bad cold.

How bad? It *killed* him.

Sammy and Dawkins quietly appeared behind us. Dawkins muttered, "This is the way the world will end: not with a bang but an . . . ah-choo."

"Gesundheit," I said at the same time Greta said, "God bless."

"I wasn't *really* sneezing." Dawkins pointed at the television. "I was suggesting that this man's sickness is yet another symptom of the world spinning off-kilter. This virus, the record-breaking heat wave that has left the entire planet dry as tinder—these are the first signs of a coming apocalypse."

"He's joking, right?" I asked my mom. "A *cold*? Isn't the end of the world supposed to have, like, explosions? Tidal waves and earthquakes?"

"The Great Influenza of 1918 killed nearly one hundred million people," Dawkins said, walking over and turning the television off. "All thanks to a little cold virus . . . and the Bend Sinister."

"The second reason is closer to home . . ." My mom touched an old silver locket she wore around her neck. "Our patient has taken a turn for the worse. She's dying."

The locket belonged to Flavia, the comatose Pure woman, and I knew it held pictures of her two kids. I didn't know her, or them, or anything else about her life. All I knew was that she was a mom, and that she must have loved her kids a ton to carry their pictures around in a necklace like that. If they were anything like me, they were probably going crazy with worry. She'd just disappeared. I looked at my own mom and felt a familiar twinge of anxiety. I knew what those kids were feeling. "So what do we do?"

"Our only hope to save her," my mom said, "and to set the world back in balance, is to retrieve Flavia's soul and restore it to her body."

"And fast," Dawkins said. "Our doctor estimates she's got a week. Probably less."

I felt queasy. Things just kept getting worse. "How'd you find him?" I asked. "Dad."

"Your mum dangled some bait she knew Truelove would snap at," Dawkins said.

I felt warm all of a sudden—angry, ashamed, and afraid all at once. Truelove is my dad's last name. Mine, too, obviously. "What bait?"

"The situation is dire, honey," my mom said. "I had to use something he wants so badly he'd risk exposure to get it."

"There's nothing he wants that bad," I said. I grew up with my dad, and even I couldn't think of anything he cared about that much.

Behind my mom was a computer with a familiar log-in screen: a gamer board I hung out on called ILZ. Or I should say, *used* to hang out on; when we arrived at Wilson Peak, we were ordered to close our Facebook profiles, delete our email addresses, and ditch all our old contacts.

"There is *one* thing," my mom said.

"Why are you logged on to ILZ?" I asked, confused. "How do you even *know* about ILZ? Is that the bait? A gamer site?"

My mom just stared at me. "The ILZ site isn't the bait."

"It's you, Ronan." Dawkins rested his hand on my shoulder. "*You're* the bait."

Half an hour later, my mom spilled a half-dozen sabers onto our dining table. We'd argued about Dad the whole walk from the lodge to our bungalow.

"What is it you want, Ronan? Do you want me to apologize for lying to your father? Because I'm not going to do that." She quickly slid each sword from its scabbard and examined the cutting edge before slamming it home again. "Yes, I went behind your back and used your old logins. I pretended to be you in order to bait your dad. And it *worked*. I'm not sorry."

"You could have asked." I pushed her the rolled-up leather wrap that held her throwing knives. "What does he even want with me?"

She untied the bundle and spread it out so that the dozen blades were all visible. "The same thing I want with you, kiddo: we love you." She removed one of the knives and pointed it at me. "A parent creates a kid and then loves that kid—even when he's being astonishingly annoying."

"But he told his flunky to kill me," I said. "At Mourner's Mouth."

"People don't always make sense, Ronan." Shoving the knife back, she rolled up the bundle and retied it. "He loves you, but he loves himself more: he was in a hurry to escape, and you got in his way." She yanked the knot tight. "Also, I seem to recall you hitting him in the face with a dustpan."

I grinned a little. "Yeah, he didn't like that much."

"I bet." She slung the swords and the knife wrap into an open duffel. "He expects you in Minneapolis in two days. So Mr. Sustermann and I and a half-dozen Guard are going there early to lay a trap. We will catch him, and we will retrieve Flavia's soul." She touched the locket.

"You think he's just, like, carrying her soul around with him?" I asked.

"Watch your tone, Evelyn," my mom said. She zipped the bag shut.

She uses my first name only when she's mad at me. "I just don't think it sounds like a very good plan," I said, so that I wouldn't say what was really bothering me.

"It's not," she admitted. "But it's the only one we have. If it doesn't work out, everything will depend on Ogabe. He is undertaking his own mission while we try this gambit."

I wanted to ask about Ogabe, but I couldn't stop myself from blurting, "You used me. To trap Dad. It's totally like something *he* would do."

"Oh, Ronan—it's *not* like that at all," she said, holding me at arm's length. "This is much bigger than you. Or me. Or your dad. What matters is Flavia, and Greta, and other innocents. Sometimes events are going to seem to be about you personally, but you have to trust me, they never are."

"I understand that," I said. "Honest, I do. But what I don't get is why you're not bringing me with you."

She picked up her bag. "Because you have an important mission of your own."

"A weekend of tests," I said, looking away. "Some mission."

"Maybe you'll do well. What's the prize?"

"A scholarship," I grumbled. "Big whoop."

She laughed. "See me off, son of mine?"

I walked her out of our bungalow and to the little central park, and stood next to Dawkins and Bentley while she, Greta's dad, and a half-dozen other Blood Guard loaded up two of the beat-up vans.

Mr. Sustermann and Greta talked quietly and hugged, then Greta came over, sniffing and wiping her eyes. "Stop staring, freak," she said. "It's rude."

Ogabe crouched down and talked intently to Sammy, who nodded again and again, finally shaking the big man's hand before leaving him and joining us.

It took about ten minutes to load the vans, and then everyone took off—first the two vans with my mom, Mr. Sustermann, and the other Blood Guard, and then, a few moments later, Ogabe in a third van, alone. He followed the single-lane road that was the only way on or off the mountain, took a turn, and disappeared.

"Where's he going?" Sammy asked Dawkins.

"Elsewhere," Dawkins said, turning away. "Come on, you lot." On the steps of the gazebo two zippered black bags waited: Dawkins' luggage.

"What now?" I asked.

"You all will pack, we will load up the McDermott's car, and then we will head down the mountain," Dawkins said.

"It's nine thirty now; we should be on the road by eleven, if we're going to reach the testing site before sundown."

Bentley ran up and dropped a green ball at our feet. She whined until Greta tossed it across the grass.

"I can't believe we're actually leaving," Greta said.

Bentley trotted back, something white clenched in her jaws. I recognized it right away: my commemorative baseball. "Come here, girl," I said, and she let me take it from her.

I wiped it clean of slobber. The seams were split, and the leather was halfway off. The guts—a rubbery wad of glued thread—were coming out one end. *Maybe I can restitch it*, I thought, trying to push the core back into the cover. As I did, I felt a slit in the rubberized guts and turned it over.

There was a slot like on a piggy bank in the center.

"Jack," I said. "This is weird."

He took the ball, peered into the slot, and said, "Interesting." Reaching into his pocket, he produced a swiss army knife, wedged the blade into the slot, and pushed. A black metal box fell out.

Dawkins folded the blade away. "Where did this baseball come from, Ronan?"

"My mom took it with her when she left our old house," I said. "She knew we weren't coming back, and she knew it meant a lot to me." I picked up the leather cover. "My dad gave it to me when I was ten."

Dawkins frowned. "That's what I was afraid of." He nudged the black box with the toe of his sneaker. "A tracking device. Even the Blood Guard missed this one. It was hidden well."

"What's that noise?" Greta asked, looking around.

I heard it, too. A buzzing in the air. "Bugs?" I said.

"No," Dawkins said. "That sound is man-made."

"Over there," Sammy said, pointing the direction the white vans had gone.

Floating slowly up the road was something thin and black and about as big around as a card table. It hovered fifteen feet in the air, held aloft by propellers at each corner.

"It's a quad copter drone," Sammy said. "I didn't know the Blood Guard had any drones."

"We don't," Dawkins said. "Everyone, let's calmly make our way to the safety of the lodge."

But it was obvious we wouldn't make it. The copter cut across the corner of the park and zoomed down the lane toward the lodge. As it passed, we could see it more clearly. Mounted on its top was a shiny chrome sphere as big as a volleyball. The air around it seemed to wiggle and warp like the air over a campfire.

"What's that silver globe thing?" Greta asked.

Near the lodge, the drone hovered. A loud electric whine began, louder than the buzz of its propellers, and tiny sparks started to snap off the globe and into the air.

Dawkins shaded his eyes and said, "It looks like a Van de Graaf generator . . . oh, bother. Everyone get down!" He pushed Greta and Sammy to the grass. I crouched, too, grabbing Bentley and pulling her close.

Just then enormous arcs of white lightning crackled out from the sphere in a dozen directions. They seared trails across the concrete, left burning zigzags in the dry grass of the park, and set the nearest cabins and trees aflame. With a final loud *whomp* of electrical discharge that made my hair stand straight up, the copter stopped working and clattered to the ground sixty feet away.

"What *was* that?" Sammy asked, crouching in the grass.

The old, tinder-dry buildings of the town caught fast. Within moments, both sides of the street were on fire, tiny flakes of ash pattering down around us like rain.

"*That* was the Bend Sinister," Dawkins said. "They're coming."

CHAPTER 3

A POLITE, WELL-DRESSED MONSTROSITY

"They're coming *here*?" I asked. The leafy tops of two trees on the far side of the park exploded into flames and a hot breeze ruffled our hair. "Didn't everyone just go to trap them?"

"I fear that was a bit of Bend Sinister misdirection," Dawkins said. He took a smartphone from his pocket and tapped at it. "We've been played."

"So are you calling Ogabe and everyone else back?" Sammy asked.

"I wish. No—this phone is useless now." He flung it into the bushes, and then pulled a yellow notebook and pen from his back pocket and scribbled a note. "That bug in the baseball? It means they've known all along where we are. So they lured the Blood Guard away, and then sent up that copter."

"But the bolts didn't touch us," Greta said. "The copter just sort of exploded."

"Precisely," Dawkins said. "And when it did, it created an electromagnetic pulse just big enough to fry the electronics in our phones and computers, like a man-made lightning strike. Likely took out everything in town." He went down on one knee and whistled softly, and Bentley trotted over. Tearing the page from his notebook, he wrapped the paper around her collar, then leaned in close, whispered something, and kissed her on her snout.

"We need to hide," Greta said.

Bentley spun and galloped straight down the road between the burning buildings. As we watched, one of the trees creaked and fell into the street, sending a curlicue of embers up into the air.

"Bentley's running straight into the worst of it!" Sammy said.

"I warned her to be careful," Dawkins said, standing and heading back to the gazebo. "She's carrying a note for the McDermott and the others. The stables are back there; they can take the horses and Bentley down the back trail."

Seeing the shocked look on Greta's face, Dawkins added, "Yes, Greta—of course there is another route off the mountain."

"I knew it!" she said, grinning despite everything. "So how do we get there?"

The wind around us was growing fierce as the surging flames sucked up oxygen.

"*We* don't. You three will have to find another way out of here."

"We *four*, you mean," Greta said.

"No, I mean *three*. The Bend Sinister will have stayed out of range of that electromagnetic pulse—a five- or ten-minute drive away. But they're likely on their way here now." Dawkins turned to me. "Ronan, you, Sammy, and Greta need to get out of here pronto." He didn't have to add, *Greta's a Pure. I'm relying on you to protect her*.

"No way," Greta said. "We're not leaving you by yourself!"

"Somebody must cover your retreat," Dawkins said. "As a Blood Guard Overseer, that task falls to me."

"We should be armed," I said.

He caught my eye and nodded, then rooted around in his bag and drew out an edgeless dueling blade that I'd learned was called a smallsword. It was about a yard long and as thin and light as a needle. "Try not to put out your eye," he said, handing it to me.

"You should probably arm me, too," Sammy said.

"Oh, should I?" Dawkins asked, and then said, "I don't have much, I'm afraid." He produced a familiar-looking slingshot. It had a wrist brace on the grip and rubber cords attached to a fat leather strip. "You remember how this works?"

"You remember the pool?" Sammy asked.

"Touché." He glanced back into the bag. "I'm afraid, Greta, that I have nothing else to spare here."

"That's okay," Greta said. "I'm happy being the brains of this trio."

"Take the ski slope; it was the best of your escape plans, Greta," Dawkins said, straightening up. We stood looking at him dumbly until he shouted, "What are you waiting for? Go! *Now!*"

Only one flattened box was still sitting at the top of the ski slope, its corner flapping in the hot gusts of air from the fire.

"Where's mine?" Sammy said, breathing hard from our run down the street.

Far away downhill was a light patch of tan that might have been Sammy's box.

"No big deal," Greta said. "We can sled down together on Ronan's box."

But the minute she and Sammy sat down, it was clear the box wasn't going anywhere. Our combined weight was just too much.

"This *so* isn't going to work," Sammy said.

"No, it won't," I agreed. Then I remembered something Dawkins had said. "But I know what will. Grab the box and come on."

Next to the boarded-up building everyone called the storehouse was a machine the size of a tractor trailer with the word ICE written in huge red letters along its side. It dispensed blocks of ice as big as suitcases—for the old iceboxes people used before refrigerators, I guess. On one end of the machine was a chute and a wire cage to catch the ice blocks as they slid from the machine.

I yanked on the big metal lever, and a block of ice slid out of the machine into the cage with a *thunk*. Sammy and I lifted that block out, and then two more after Greta pulled the lever.

"These things weigh a ton," Sammy said.

"That's what the box is for," I said.

It was almost easy to drag the ice back to the top of the slope using the sheet of cardboard. We slid the blocks off and sat down.

Immediately the seat of my jeans soaked through with cold.

Half the town was on fire behind us. There was so much smoke in the sky that the light had grown dim and weird, like twilight at ten in the morning.

"Time to go," I said.

"We can't do this," Greta said, standing up again.

"It's just a little bit of water!" I said.

"Not that," Greta snapped. "*Jack!* We can't just run away and leave Jack by himself."

"Seriously, dude," Sammy said, picking up a stone and loading it into his sling. "We're supposed to be in this together."

I didn't want to abandon Dawkins, either. But my mission as a Blood Guard was to safeguard my charge—Greta. I could never explain to her that we weren't running away, we were protecting a Pure: her. If I insisted that we leave Dawkins, she'd want to know *why*, and I didn't have an answer for that.

"You're right," I said, standing up. I was never going to make it as a Blood Guard. I couldn't even stop a Pure from running straight into danger. "Let's rescue Jack."

Too late. We reached the park just as a black SUV was pulling up.

Before we could be spotted, I dropped to my hands and knees, and signaled to Greta and Sammy to get down, too. We crawled up behind a low hedge at the south end of the park.

Dawkins was slouched against the gazebo, his arms crossed, looking bored. Beside him, a sword was planted point-first in the ground.

Three people climbed out of the SUV—two men with short dark hair, and a woman with her brown hair pulled into a ponytail. Two of them wore sword belts; I could see the shiny pommels as they walked. The second man had a Tesla rifle slung across his back. I'd never seen these people before, but I recognized their tailored suits and blank expressions: Bend Sinister agents. They moved in the same silent, precise way as the team that had supported Ms. Hand, the woman who'd done her best to kill us back in June.

"Where's their Hand?" I whispered just as the back door on the SUV slid aside.

The man who got out was the biggest person I'd ever seen in my life. He was tall, sure, but also monstrously fat. His body swelled out from his triple chins to his round, wide waist before tapering back the other way to his dainty little feet. Or maybe he just looked enormous because of his white suit, which sort of made him glow like the moon. Next to him, the three Bend Sinister agents looked like shrimpy little kids playing dress up.

One of the agents reached into the car and handed a white-tipped black cane and a white bowler to the man, who gently placed it atop his head.

The Hand's three agents slowly fanned out across the grass in a half circle with the fat man at its center. Each swept his or her head slowly back and forth, like a surveillance camera.

"What are they doing?" Greta whispered.

The man waddled forward, a phony smile on his face. "We didn't expect to find a welcoming committee, Mr. Dawkins."

"Come find out just how welcoming I can be." Dawkins grinned and opened his arms wide.

"Ah, thank you, but I'd rather keep my distance." The man laughed politely, then placed his right hand on his chest. "The name is Patch Steiner. A pleasure to meet the notorious Jack Dawkins at last."

"Yes, yes—I get that a lot." Dawkins picked something up off the gazebo's railing—the rubbery core of the baseball. "But I must say, it's a surprise to meet a blind Hand."

"Oh, Mr. Dawkins, I may be blind, but I can see much better than you!" The man snapped his fingers, and his smile changed—it got toothier and meaner somehow. "All I need do is borrow your eyesight."

Dawkins tilted his head and blinked, then swept his hand back and forth in front of his eyes.

"How does it feel?" Steiner asked, walking forward. "To be blind and helpless?"

"I'm hardly *helpless*," Dawkins said. He snapped his wrist and the baseball core arced straight into Patch Steiner's gut. "I don't need to be able to *see* you to *hit* you. Then again, you are a very large target." Dawkins closed his eyes, drew the sword out of the ground, and took a defensive stance.

"Much as I enjoy toying with you, Mr. Dawkins," Steiner said, wiping his forehead with a handkerchief, "I've actually come for the boy. The one who belongs to Head Truelove."

I must have gasped, because Greta elbowed me.

Steiner clucked. "Did you send the children away to safety? If so, we'll catch them. I've left agents at the foot of the road as well as on that trail down the back of the mountain—yes, we know about that escape route." Steiner turned away, signaling his team forward. "A pity we don't have an audience. Two, please cut Mr. Dawkins up into tiny pieces."

One of the Bend Sinister agents raised his sword.

Sammy stood up. "That's enough," he announced to

no one in particular. Stretching the slingshot band back the length of his arm, he let fly.

The stone struck the Bend Sinister agent so hard his feet left the ground as he fell backward.

"One down," Sammy said, putting another rock into his sling. "The fat guy's next."

I didn't hear what he said after that, because I was already charging across the park, my sword drawn, running at the woman.

"Why, Evelyn Truelove!" Patch Steiner cried, sounding like I was a dearly beloved, long-lost friend. "You are the reason—ah!"

Sammy's second rock had scored a bull's-eye. Steiner reeled back dazed, his hands to his head.

The woman's face was blank, almost bored-looking, as she raised her weapon—a heavy cavalry sword. My small-sword was next to useless against that.

So, as I ran, I whipped my blade straight at her and let go.

But a sword isn't a dart, and it doesn't fly like one. Mine spun end over end and smacked her in the shoulder hilt-first. It was just enough to throw her off balance, and it bought me just enough time to drop into a slide like a runner stealing second.

I rammed straight into her legs and she came down on top of me, dropping her sword. It spun out of reach on the grass.

I shoved her off, rolled over, and grabbed her weapon, then pointed it at her as I got up.

She got up, too. Her jaw dropped open and she screamed—no words, just a strangled noise that made my skin crawl. And then, even though she was completely unarmed, she flung out her hands and lunged at me.

The world went dark.

Not dark like a cloud going in front of the sun, but dark like every light everywhere in the universe had been snuffed out forever. I couldn't see at all.

Steiner wasn't dazed any longer: he'd stolen my eyesight.

But I'd already started reacting before going blind—stepping back and to the left, raising the sword to defend myself. I didn't see what happened next, though I *heard* it—a wet, ripping sound. And I *felt* it—a weight on the blade wrenching it downward.

She had leaped straight onto my sword.

Shocked, I let go and stumbled, then tripped and landed on my back.

A Tesla gun discharged—I heard the familiar crackle of electricity and the air filled with a metallic burning stink that overpowered even the smell of wood smoke. Whoever it was fired off a second and a third bolt. There was a long noise of metal and glass shrieking and popping, the sounds of serious destruction.

I rolled over on the grass and covered my head.

Dawkins shouted, "Give me that!" I heard a smack and a bit of scuffling, and then he added, "Only a coward brings a gun to a knife fight."

A hand seized mine.

"It's me, Greta." She helped me up. "Stealing your sight only works if your eyes are open, right? So try closing them."

Smart. "Good idea," I said, shutting my eyes.

"All of your agents are down, Steiner," Dawkins said as Greta led me to him. So enough of your little sensory-stealing parlor trick—we all don't need to be able to see in order to test this Tesla gun on *you*. Get out of Ronan's head."

"As you wish," Steiner said, and suddenly I could detect a glow again through my eyelids.

I opened my eyes and saw Dawkins aiming the Tesla rifle at Patch Steiner, who was lying on his back on the grass. His hat had been knocked off, and he had a welt on his forehead—Sammy's work. "But you leave me blind—you've subdued my agents, and they usually act as my eyes."

"Oh, boo hoo. You have two other agents guarding the roads. Borrow *their* eyesight for a while."

With a muffled boom, one of the burning bungalows collapsed on itself, sparks spewing into the air. I flinched.

"We really need to get out of here," Greta said.

I glanced at the black SUV the Bend Sinister had brought with them, but it looked like it had been sawed in half. By one of the stray Tesla shots, I guessed. "We can't take their car."

"What do we do with him?" Sammy asked, pointing at Steiner.

Steiner glanced around wildly. "Come now—I can't hurt you; I can't even get to my feet." He rolled back and forth like a turtle on its back. "You wouldn't leave me to burn in this fire, would you?"

"We can't arrest you," Dawkins said, wiping his sword and replacing it in its scabbard, "and carrying someone of your magnificent girth will be impossible, so you're just going to have to . . ."

Finger to his lips, Dawkins led the three of us at a jog across the grass.

"To *what*, Mr. Dawkins?" Steiner shouted out. "Where are you?"

We broke into a flat-out run as Dawkins said to himself, "To find your own way out of this hell."

CHAPTER 4
KOALAKLUB? KOALAKLUB!

Just as we rounded the corner toward the ski slope, the world went wobbly.

The sounds around me—the roar and crackle of the fires blazing behind us, the smack of our feet against the pavement—all of it went watery and strange. I couldn't hear anything over the pounding of the blood in my ears, and suddenly I couldn't find my balance, either, like my body had forgotten which way was up or down.

The horizon rolled and the ground rose like a wave in front of me.

The four of us were running hard, and I barely got my hands up before I slammed against the road.

The sounds of the world rushed back in, but when I tried to stand, I couldn't make my arms and legs behave, and I fell right over again.

"Jack!" Greta shouted. "Something's wrong with Ronan!"

Dawkins ran back to me. "Can you hear me, Ronan?" he shouted.

"I'm not deaf," I said. "I just can't stand up for some reason."

"That grotesquerie back there is messing about with your inner ear and trashing your balance." He leaned over me and said, "I'm going to carry you, Ronan. Try not to vomit on me."

"I'm not going to throw up!" I protested.

"Don't get touchy—it's a common side effect of sudden balance disorders." Dawkins grabbed my arms, yanked them up, and draped me over his shoulder. And then we were galloping again.

With each stride, my gut bounced against his shoulder. Pretty soon it was all I could do not to cough up my breakfast.

So I thought about my parents. My dad obviously knew I wasn't going to meet him in Minneapolis, and my mom's plan to catch him was doomed. Was my dad waiting there to ambush my mom and the rest of the Blood Guard? Is that why he'd sent this Patch Steiner guy to fetch me, because he couldn't be here?

My mom was heading into a trap.

We had to warn her.

I opened my mouth to say so and realized that it was a bad idea.

"You're looking a tiny bit green," Dawkins said, sliding me to the ground. "But you made it. Now take some deep breaths. The worst is yet to come."

"We only have three ice blocks," Sammy said, grabbing our cardboard. "I'll go get another one."

"No time," Dawkins said. "Ronan and I will ride down together."

"How?" I mumbled. I barely fit onto the ice block before. I tried to stand but the ground came up and caught me.

"On my lap, you big baby," Dawkins said. He sat on one of the blocks and then dragged me over so that my back was to his chest and my legs between his. He wrapped his arms tightly around me. "This is going to be *fun*."

Moments later, we were flying.

Okay, not really.

Not, like, soaring through the clouds with our arms stuck out and our capes snapping in the air behind us like some sort of goofy superheroes.

But that's totally what it *felt* like.

Except for Dawkins' nonstop chortling.

We shot down the slope so fast that wind whistled in my ears and blew back my hair and pushed its way into my lungs so that breathing out was something I had to think about.

But at least I wasn't feeling sick anymore.

And then our ice block started to spin, the trees swirling around us in a dark blur, and I felt sick in an entirely new way. We ended up facing backward, looking uphill at the top of the mountain. It was wreathed in fiery light.

I hoped Bentley, the McDermott, and the others had managed to get to safety.

And then we shot over a little rise and high into the air. For a dizzying half second, we were aloft and weightless and really flying.

It might even have been cool if not for one hard truth: we had to come back down.

Dawkins hugged me tight and twisted himself around so that he hit the ground first. The impact broke us apart. I rolled a good twenty feet before I stopped.

I woozily stood up. I was covered in dirt and grass, and I had burrs in my hair, but I had control of my limbs again. Whatever grip Steiner had on my balance had disappeared—I guess his power had a limited range.

Five hundred feet farther downhill, where the slope flattened out, Greta and Sammy were waiting. We were close enough to see the knotty mess of Greta's red hair and Sammy's huge grin. They waved and I waved back.

"That was fun, wasn't it?" Dawkins asked.

Fun? Maybe if I hadn't been carried like a baby all the way down, if my mom and Greta's dad weren't in danger, if my dad wasn't coming for me and everyone I cared about. Maybe if I had been any use whatsoever in that fight instead of someone who had to be rescued again and again. "No," I said. "That wasn't fun at all."

"Ronan, you should *not* have come back for me." Dawkins raised his hand to stop me from responding. "You endangered Greta. The first commandment of the Blood Guard is to protect the Pure."

"But that's exactly *why* we came back," I said. "*Greta.*

She wouldn't let me leave you behind, and I didn't know how to keep her safe without her figuring out what she is. I can't lie to her—she's way too smart."

Dawkins bit his lip. "A fair point. Greta poses a difficulty for us that I failed to take fully into account." He grimaced. "Anyway, had you three not come back, Gargantua back there? He would have used me as a chew toy. So, thanks for that."

"No problem," I said.

"Just don't do it again. When I tell you to *run*, you go full tilt as fast and as far as you can. Understand?"

"Understood," I said.

We jogged along the bank of a creek until we came upon a dirt road, pausing only so Dawkins could unsling the Tesla rifle and toss it into the water. "Vile things," he said, before breaking again into a run.

"Are we going to meet up with the McDermott and the others?" I asked.

"No," Dawkins said. "That Steiner chap said he had agents on the back path, so joining them would be dangerous. Besides, those old Guard can take care of themselves, while we make good our escape via the US Forest Service."

I didn't know what the Forest Service had to do with anything, but I was too winded to ask.

The road took us under the trees, and we could no longer see Wilson Peak, couldn't even see the dirty smoke anymore. Down here, it was almost like the fire hadn't happened. I knew better, of course—if Patch Steiner had survived the fire, he was probably already on the phone to my dad, explaining how I'd escaped, carried off the mountain by Dawkins like a baby in a Bjorn.

"Obviously we're going to warn our parents, right?" Greta asked.

"And Ogabe," Sammy added.

"And then we'll go help them," I finished.

We'd reached a clearing. In front of us was a one-room wooden cabin only a little bigger than a shed. There was a closed door and a single dusty window.

"We will warn them, yes," Dawkins said. "But help them out? No. The last thing they need is for me to show up with a truckful of unruly teenagers."

"I'm not an unruly teenager," Sammy pointed out.

That was true. He was only eleven.

"Said *precisely* like an unruly teenager," Dawkins replied, leading us around the cabin, "and thereby proving my point."

A mud-splattered pickup truck was parked on the other side. A golden US Forest Service medallion as big as a plate glinted on the hood. Dawkins yanked on the driver's side door, and it opened with a screech.

"We will send word about what happened, we will warn the Guard, and we will continue with our mission. You three will sit for the tests that make up the Glass Gauntlet"—we all groaned, but Dawkins ignored us—"while I locate the Damascene 'Scope. It's key if we're to save Flavia."

"No way," Greta said. "Bad enough you kept us captive on a mountain all summer, but now you're telling us we can't go help my dad and Ronan's mom? Forget it."

"Greta, first: I don't know the address of the meet up, so we couldn't join them even if I thought doing so was a good idea, which I do not." He flipped down the driver's side visor. A set of keys fell to the floor mat. "And second: I can think of no safer hideaway from the Bend Sinister than a nondescript testing facility, the three of you penciling in bubbles on answer sheets. No one will look for you there."

"Are you going to steal this truck?" Greta asked.

"*Please*—the ranger is another retired Guard." Dawkins rattled the keys. "He'd *want* us to use his vehicle. Let's see what else he may have left for us."

Inside the cabin was a cot, a sink, and a desk with a massive old laptop that looked about as heavy as a phone book.

"Not state-of-the-art," Dawkins said, grabbing the laptop and handing it to Sammy, "but filchers can't be choosers."

"Probably no Internet out here," Sammy said, dragging out the power cord.

"Probably not." Dawkins opened each of the drawers, said, "Ah ha!" and took out a bright orange cell phone. Its center button was an exclamation point. "An emergency mobile. Excellent!"

"What a relief," Greta said. "Call for help."

He pressed the button and listened. "Not surprisingly,

there's no cell phone coverage out here, either. But it wouldn't matter anyway, as I don't have the numbers for the new Blood Guard–issued smartphones."

"You didn't memorize them?" Greta said.

"What is this, the twentieth century? Who memorizes phone numbers anymore?" He pocketed the phone. "Still, this will come in handy." Then he leaned over and wrote something on the dusty desk blotter:

KOALALOU

"What's that mean?" I asked.

He ignored me. "Enough dilly-dallying! It's time we made good our escape."

But the truck wouldn't start. Though Dawkins cranked the key in the ignition, the engine made no noise whatsoever.

"Another impressive getaway," Greta muttered from the passenger seat.

"Should we get out and push?" Sammy suggested from the jump seat behind her.

Dawkins raised a finger. "Almost forgot!" He slipped out of the cab, went around to the US Forest Service medallion, and wrenched it off the hood. He moved it a foot and a half closer to the windshield, and it reattached itself with a heavy *thunk*.

"What was that all about?" I asked as he got back in.

"Primitive theft deterrent," Dawkins said, turning the keys. The engine quietly rumbled to life. "There are massive magnets in that medallion—powerful enough to activate an interlock in the engine. Otherwise any dodo who came across this truck could steal it, and then it wouldn't have been here for *us*."

Dawkins gunned the truck along the dirt roads like he knew where he was going, and he eventually turned onto a two-lane street that led to a highway.

"Is the Bend Sinister following us?" I asked.

"Undoubtedly," he said. "However, they probably think we're still bushwhacking our way off the mountain. I just pray we are far away before they realize their mistake."

"And then once we find phone coverage," Greta said, "you're going to call for help?"

Dawkins snorted. "Call whom? The Blood Guard has only one hundred and forty-four core members—four to watch over each of the Thirty-Six. Those Guard are in deep cover, meaning we can't risk exposing their identities to the Bend Sinister."

"But there must be *somebody* else," Sammy said. "That can't be everyone."

"There are also nine Overseers, including Ogabe and yours truly, as well as one Grand Architect, whose work I must keep a secret even from you. On top of that, we have several dozen retired Guard and a few trusted confidants, but . . . that's the lot of us. We don't have a budget, or a headquarters, or a monthly newsletter, or even a blog—just a few hundred of us scattered around the world."

None of us said anything, just sat and stared out at the shadowy trees and listened to the hum of the tires on the pavement. We were somewhere on the western border of Virginia, far away from anyone else, the only car on the road.

"We are totally outnumbered," Greta whispered. "They could be all around us."

"We should try my mom's old email address—" I started to say.

"Terminated months ago."

"She might still have her old phone," I said.

"Left behind in Brooklyn."

"So how are we going to let them know they're heading into a trap?" Sammy asked.

"The Blood Guard *does* have one secret avenue through which we can post messages," Dawkins said, "a channel hidden in an innocuous website. By any chance have you ever heard of . . . KoalaKlub?"

Sammy's eyebrows rose. "That crappy old website? That thing's been gone since forever."

"Maybe not as gone as you think," Dawkins said.

"What is it?" I asked.

"It was this early attempt at a sort of Minecraft game site," Sammy explained. "Except players were blocky koalas instead of people, and the building options were super-limited. The koalas made houses in caves—"

"*Treehouses*," Dawkins corrected. "They didn't live in caves! That'd be barbaric!"

"Whatever," Sammy said, rolling his eyes. "*Treehouses*. It doesn't matter. The whole site sucked so bad that it closed down in, like, 2001."

"2008," Dawkins muttered. "It went bankrupt in 2008."

"Why?" Greta asked.

"Because apparently teenagers and adults didn't want to pretend to be digital koala bears—who knew?" Dawkins shrugged.

"Now it's one of those legendary lousy sites," Sammy said. "Like FaceSpace, only nowhere near that big."

"I don't think that's what that site was called," Greta said.

"After it closed down," Dawkins said, "the Blood Guard bought the programming for a song and hid our secret chat channel within the old website. Anyone not in the know thinks they've stumbled upon a shut-down, defunct game site from the turn of the century."

"Another Blood Guard ghost town," Greta said.

"Exactly," Dawkins said. "If the Guard needs to communicate, we just show up and see who else is there. No other users are allowed into the virtual world."

"But what if no other Blood Guard users are there?" Greta asked.

Dawkins shrugged. "Then we leave notes in our main treehouse—virtual signposts that help us get in contact with the others in case of emergency."

"You're telling us that the only way to contact the Blood Guard is through an out-of-business web game?" I asked.

"Unfortunately, at the moment, yes," Dawkins said. "When we fail to answer our dead phones, your mom, Greta's father, and Ogabe will know to check the KoalaKlub treehouse. So we need to find a safe place to log on and get KoalaLou to that treehouse pronto. We'll write out the number of this emergency cell phone using the wooden blocks in KoalaLou's playpen."

"Wooden blocks?" Greta said. "You have got to be joking."

"Good point," Dawkins said, nodding. "The carton of sidewalk chalk in KoalaLou's kitchen will be far easier—we won't have to hunt for numbers that way."

"That's not what I meant!" Greta said.

Three hours later, the four of us were crowded around the old laptop at the back of a coffee shop in a minimall outside Washington, DC.

Dawkins tore a sheet of paper from his yellow notebook, wrote a web address, user name, and password on it, and handed it to Sammy. "You're sure you can set up a safe link?"

"Easy," Sammy said, typing strings of text into the laptop. "Just give me a second to set up a secure connection and . . . we're in."

KoalaKlub turned out to be like a low-rent version of Minecraft, but with really clunky, candy-colored graphics. Our chunky avatar, KoalaLou, materialized in the central square of a funky little town filled with frozen koalas. A dozen of them were scattered around, their heads drooped, looking like they were asleep.

"What's with those other koalas?" I asked.

"Those are just empty avatars from when there were actual players in this game," Dawkins said

"*This* is the Blood Guard's backup communication system?" Greta asked, sagging back in her chair. "Seriously?"

"More like our backup, backup, backup communication system," Dawkins said. "But yes, it *does* look pretty silly, I will grant you that."

"I think it's sort of crazy smart," Sammy said. "I mean, if you were looking for a secret society, the last place you'd think to look would be in a closed-off online game."

"I guess that's true," I said, watching Sammy pilot the avatar to her home on the edge of the virtual town.

We turned out to be the only koala in the treehouse, so Dawkins left a message in pink chalk on the gray kitchen floor.

BEND TRAP! CALL!

—J.D.

And then the number of the emergency cell phone.

"That's it?" Greta asked.

"That's all we can do for the moment," Dawkins said. "I'm sure someone will respond by tomorrow morning."

"And if no one does?" I asked, wondering if my mom and the Blood Guard were going to stop in the middle of their mission to check out a defunct website.

"If we haven't heard from anyone by tomorrow morning," Dawkins said, powering down the laptop, "then I will take more drastic measures."

"Such as what?" Greta asked.

"I haven't figured that out yet," Dawkins said. "But you can count on my measures being so drastically drastic that they will make more run-of-the-mill drastic measures quake in shame and terror." He licked his lips. "Until such a time, the most drastic thing I am going to suggest is that we pick up a few dozen of those doughnuts over there by the register. Who else is hungry?"

CHAPTER 5

THE PECULIAR MS. GLASS

Four hours later, Dawkins turned off the highway, taking an exit marked only with a sign that read PRIVATE. It put us onto a long, winding drive—no cars, no houses, no stores. It was only a little after five o'clock, and the sun wouldn't set for a couple of hours, but the shadows of the trees along the road made it seem later than it was.

Dawkins flicked on the headlights.

Greta said, "So tell us again: these tests we're taking—"

"The Glass Gauntlet," Dawkins said. "A series of tests."

"You're sure it's not a knight's glove?" Sammy asked. "Because that would be cool."

"Yet highly impractical," Dawkins said. "No, the name is clearly an attempt to make it sound more exciting. I mean, if they called it the Intelligent Child Exam Battery, no one would be interested, would they? Though maybe the million dollars would be an inducement."

"Million dollars?" I repeated. "You didn't tell us it's a million dollars!"

"Didn't I? Must have forgotten during the burning down of our town and the mad flight for our lives from that white-suited monster. Anyway, yes, the winner is awarded a million-dollar prize."

"Why is the scholarship so high?" Greta asked. "No university costs that much."

"It's prize money *and* a scholarship. And some sort of lifelong apprenticeship with Glass Industries."

"Are these like the tests we take in school?" I asked. "History, math, reading comprehension?"

"Haven't the foggiest," Dawkins said. "When word came about the Damascene 'Scope having turned up—well, we seized whatever excuse we could find to sneak onto the Glass Industries estate. This obscure competition seemed our best shot. I will be your chaperone to these exams, and will skulk around while you bubble in circles on test forms. Though fair warning: as soon as I find the Damascene 'Scope, I'm grabbing you and we are taking off."

"What is this 'Scope thing?" I asked.

"A rather dangerous experimental Blood Guard device." Dawkins frowned. "The Victorians christened it the Damascene Achromatic Animascope, which is such an ugly mouthful of syllables that most people just call it the Damascene 'Scope. It was destroyed a hundred and fifty years ago, by order of the Grand Architect, and its pieces scattered so it could never be used again."

"But if it was destroyed, how come we're going to get it now?" Sammy asked.

"Because apparently someone lied," Dawkins said.

"What does it do?" Greta asked.

"The 'Scope was constructed to do two things. The first focuses the energy that radiates from a Pure's soul. Like a laser beam, that light can then be aimed at a person—a seriously bad person—and the radiance of the Pure will . . . burn away the bad person's defects. They'll be all sunshine and smiles afterward." He snapped his fingers. "That was the theory, anyway."

"Sounds kind of mad scientist-y," Sammy said.

Dawkins nodded. "Very much so. It never worked properly, and that's why the order came down to destroy it."

"So why do the Blood Guard want it now?" Greta asked.

"Because of its second, never-tested setting. Theoretically, *that* setting allows the projection of a Pure soul into a host body. Or, we hope, *back* into a host body."

I thought again of Flavia, the Pure woman my dad had left in a coma. We could undo that? "So if we can find this 'Scope thing and get it working, we can save Flavia's life?"

"Absolutely," Dawkins said. "If we can get the 'Scope, and are able to retrieve Flavia's soul, then we can save her *and* restore balance to the world. That deadly virus? These endless heat waves and wildfires? That end-of-the-world business we fret about so much? If the Damascene 'Scope works, we stop all of that cold. All by saving Flavia. She is the whole reason we're here."

Greta shook her head. "Why didn't you say that in the first place?"

The private drive dead-ended at an enormous black iron gate attached to an even higher stone wall, the kind you'd need a fireman's ladder to get over.

"Good luck climbing that," I said.

"Let's just hope we don't have to leave in a hurry," Dawkins said. He pulled alongside an intercom and pressed the CALL button.

The speaker buzzed. "Good afternoon," said a man's voice. "Are you with the Forest Service?"

Dawkins laughed and explained that he was escorting three students here for the tests, and that the truck was just a loaner, and then a moment later, the gigantic gate eased open.

On the other side of the wall, the woods had been cut away. An endless lawn rolled away from us like the world's biggest private park. Everything was a whole lot brighter and sunnier.

"All of this is for one family?" Greta asked.

"Worse," Dawkins said. "There is only one surviving member of the Glass family. Everything you see here belongs to her."

"This is all for one *person*?" Sammy whistled.

The drive snaked down the middle of the parkland, between low hills of grass dotted with clumps of trees and little stone pathways. An enormous circular lake appeared on the left, with an island in its center.

Or at least I thought it was a lake until I saw that the edges were perfectly rounded and the water a bright blue. "Is that thing a *pool*?" I asked.

"Never mind the pool," Greta said, pointing. "What's that over there?"

On the other side of the road, so far away that we couldn't really see it clearly, was a solid row of tall brown bushes. They must have been leafy once upon a time, but now they just looked like a wall of creepy dead spiny things clawing at the sky.

"Maybe that's a garden they left to die," Greta wondered. "They could be conserving water. It *has* been a hot summer."

"They're not conserving anything," I said. "Did you miss that pool back there?"

"Enough rubbernecking, you lot," Dawkins said. "We're here. Look alert."

We went over a little hill and in front of us was the main house.

Greta stared at it and frowned. "I've got a bad feeling about this place."

Of course the house was big—I expected that much. Two tall stories high, with eight fat pillars in front holding up one of those giant triangular capstones over a huge stone porch, and rows of big windows stretching across the top and bottom. It looked a lot like pictures I've seen of the White House, except for one thing:

It was jet-black. Everything but the big brass door was completely and utterly colorless.

"What kind of crazy person paints her house black?" Sammy asked.

In front of the porch, a black stone fountain jetted water high up into the air. Parked beside it were two black golf carts.

"At least the water's not black," Greta said. "That's something."

"Let's just find this 'Scope and get out of here," I said.

Dawkins pulled in next to the golf carts, and as Sammy, Greta, and I got out, he leaned over the hood and quietly moved the Forest Service medallion back to its original position.

Dawkins straightened his leather jacket and combed his fingers through his hair. "It's showtime, folks!" He led the way across the black stone porch and pressed the glowing doorbell.

A thin, young, shaven-headed man in a light gray suit opened the door. "Welcome to the Glass Gauntlet," he said. "I am Nestor, the head of operations. You three must be Samuel, Greta, and . . . Evelyn." He frowned and looked down at his clipboard. "There must be some mistake. I have two girls listed."

"*I'm* Evelyn," I said. "But everyone calls me Ronan."

"Ah, sorry!" Nestor marked up his list and then stood aside. "Well then, Ronan, Greta, and Samuel, why don't you three come inside?" To Dawkins he said, "Thank you for bringing them, driver. You may return to pick them up on Tuesday morning." He began to close the door.

"Sure thing," Dawkins said, snapping off a two-finger salute. "I'll be back bright—"

The lock clicked and cut him off.

Greta raised her eyebrows. "Is there a reason Mr. Dawkins isn't joining us?"

Nestor smiled. "The Gauntlet application was quite clear on this matter. Only students are allowed to remain on the grounds during the testing."

"But why?" I asked.

"Because we say so." His smile vanished. "Now please, come with me."

Our shoes squeaking on the checkered tile, we followed him into an enormous entry hall where a grand staircase swept up to the second story. A massive crystal chandelier glimmered overhead. At least the inside of the house wasn't painted black: The walls were gray and white, and a red carpet flowed down the stairs. A corridor ran straight back under the staircase, past a desk where a bunch of television monitors glowed.

"What's in there?" Greta asked, pointing to our left.

Over a set of double doors was a sign reading MUSEUM OF PERCEPTUAL INQUIRY.

Nestor gestured in the other direction. "You will want to wait in the sitting room, with the others."

The doors to our right opened onto a dark-paneled room packed with couches, big padded chairs, and a grand piano. In the center of the room were four red velvet–covered benches. Sitting on two of them were a teenage boy and a dark-haired woman in a navy skirt and a shimmery white blouse, wearing a string of pearls.

"Ms. Glass will join you in a moment," Nestor said, closing the doors behind us.

The woman glanced our way and wrinkled her lip, and I realized she was just a kid like us—only she was wearing makeup and jewelry and dressed like someone a lot older.

"Hi!" Greta said, sitting down across from her.

The girl sighed loudly, crossed her arms, and turned away.

"Never mind Elspeth," said the boy on the other bench. "She thinks she's better than anyone whose feet touch the ground. That is, everyone." His short brown hair stood straight up on his head, gelled into hornlike spikes. "I'm Kieran," he said. Unlike the girl, he was dressed like a normal kid—jeans and sneakers and a green hoodie.

"Nice to meet you," Greta said.

The girl named Elspeth snorted and said, "Wait until you see the face mask."

"Shut up about that," Kieran snapped. "You're gonna spoil it."

"What*ever*," Elspeth said.

I was dying to ask about that—how do you spoil a mask?—but Greta was still doing the friendly thing, introducing me and Sammy as we took a seat on the fourth bench.

"You guys don't look like much," Kieran said. "And you're, what? Ten years old?" he asked Sammy. "Aren't you afraid of getting hurt?"

"Hurt?" Greta scowled. "*How*? Paper cuts? Pencil jabs?"

"And for the record," Sammy said. "I'm eleven."

Before Kieran could reply, a toilet flushed, a door behind the piano opened, and a girl walked out. She was a shrimpy little kid whose long hair was so pale and fine she looked like she had a halo of white dandelion fuzz around her head.

"I'm Blue," she said. She looked like she was nine at the most.

"Your name is *Blue*?" Sammy asked. "For real?"

"You got a problem with that?" Blue asked, her hands making fists.

"No," Sammy said, "no problem, just think it's cool is all."

"Never mind them," Greta said, putting out her hand, but the little girl ignored it. "I'm Greta."

"Whatever." Blue was short and skinny, with bright eyes the color of her name and a silver skeleton-key pendant around her neck. She plopped down next to Elspeth.

Just then, from somewhere behind the closed doors, came the first four notes of a famous symphony.

"Beethoven's Fifth," Greta murmured.

"Doorbell," Elspeth said.

A moment later, the doors opened and Dawkins strolled in, an easy grin on his face, Nestor beside him, scowling. Blue stared at them with her mouth wide open.

". . . it's certainly not a new vehicle, if that's what you're getting at," Dawkins was saying.

"But for it to break down *now*, before you are able to leave the grounds . . . it's highly suspicious," Nestor replied.

"So you think someone here sabotaged it?" Dawkins asked. "Maybe we ought to call the police."

"An auto repairman would make more sense." Nestor pointed to one of the chairs. "Have a seat, and I'll find some way to accommodate you until we can fix your truck."

Dawkins thanked him, sank into the chair, and winked at me.

"Welcome to the Glass Gauntlet!" said a strange metallic voice.

In the doorway behind Nestor stood a squat robot no taller than Sammy. Its waist was as thick around as a metal trash can, and it was outfitted with two arms that ended in articulated hands, as well as a couple of other armlike appendages. It rolled forward on two triangular tank treads until it was in the center of the room, the chrome sphere of its head spinning around every few seconds, bunches of lenses focusing on each of us in turn.

"I am your host," the robot said. "You may call me Ms. Glass."

CHAPTER 6

THE MUSEUM OF PERCEPTUAL INQUIRY

"You're Ms. Glass?" I said. "But you're a robot."

"You must forgive my not being able to meet with you in person," came the voice from the robot's central grill, "but I am recovering from an illness and must avoid children—who, as everyone knows, are walking petri dishes of viruses, bacteria, and casually-picked-up terminal diseases."

"I am not a walking petri dish!" Greta protested.

Rings of red LEDs around the robot's lenses lit up like raised eyebrows. "Nothing personal, of course."

"Couldn't you just use, like, Skype?" asked Sammy. "That'd be less weird, right?"

"Allow me to apologize for the children," Elspeth said, standing and sweeping her arm out to indicate the rest of us.

"Apologize for yourself, snob," Kieran said. "We didn't do nothing wrong."

"Please excuse all of us," Dawkins said. "None of us were expecting you to be so, so, um—"

"Robotic?" the robot asked. The head spun and a bundle of lenses focused on Dawkins. "Who are you?"

"My name is Jack Dawkins, and I am the chaperone for—"

"You are *not* supposed to be here," the robot said. "The test is restricted to precisely a half-dozen students, chosen via—"

Dawkins interrupted. "My truck won't start."

The robot seemed to consider this, then turned back to us, saying, "Welcome, students, to the first ever Glass Gauntlet! As you know, we are seeking a student who shows a rare mix of promising talents. Intelligence! Problem-solving skills! Ingenuity! Ruthlessness!"

Next to me, Greta whispered, "Ruthlessness?"

"And physical prowess! Being smart isn't enough to conquer this world; no, you also must be strong. The Glass Gauntlet is not for the weak!

"Over the next three days," the robot went on, "you will undertake a half-dozen tests, with Mr. Nestor, and my assistant, Ms. Vaughn, acting as proctors. We know that children love games, so we have designed the most nefarious games we could imagine. All to test your mettle!"

"Wait," Greta said. "These aren't academic tests?"

But the robot either didn't hear or chose to ignore her. "We will eliminate one or more competitors after each event. Provided one of you has earned enough points

67

by Tuesday morning, you will be given the final test and emerge the victor.

"Tonight, the evening is yours. But Saturday morning, the tests begin! Guest rooms have been assigned to each of you on the second floor, and our dining room will be yours for dinner."

"What about that museum over yonder?" Dawkins asked, pointing back the way we'd come.

The robot regarded him for a moment and then said, "The western wing of the house is locked and off-limits. It is best that you all remain near the house, as well; after dark, a security detail patrols the grounds of the estate. We will not be able to protect you if you wander away on your own."

"*Protect* us?" Sammy repeated. "From what?"

"Good luck to each of you!" The robot spun on its treads and rolled back into the entry hall.

"We need to talk!" Greta hissed to Dawkins.

But he hushed her. "All in good time, Sustermann," he whispered. And then, to Nestor, "Will I be getting a room? It sounds like sleeping in the truck might be dangerous."

Nestor frowned. "I'll look into it and get back to you."

"Excellent!" Dawkins said, beaming at him. "And the robot mentioned dinner—I don't suppose you know what's on the menu?"

Nestor's frown deepened. He crossed the room, and I had a brief glimpse of a shiny wooden dining table surrounded by high-backed chairs before he closed a door behind him.

"Our Mr. Nestor doesn't seem friendly at all," Dawkins said, leading us away from the other kids, back into the entry hall. "But at least he'll be tied up for a few minutes. Will that give you enough time, Greta?"

She worked a bobby pin out of her hair, bent it, and smiled.

The doors to the Museum of Perceptual Inquiry opened onto an enormous room three times as long as the sitting room and twice as tall. It was as if all the walls had been knocked out of this side of the house to create one giant gallery. Through the windows on one side we could see the Forest Service truck in the driveway; across the room toward the back of the house another row of windows looked out across more grass—the backyard, I guessed. And in between were two aisles of dusty junk—Ms. Glass' Museum of Perceptual Inquiry.

Greta sneezed. "What is this place?"

"This Glass woman is a collector," Dawkins whispered. "Early cameras, optical devices, and magical stage items from the nineteenth century onward."

"It's awesome," Sammy said, hurrying ahead.

"Why magic?" I asked.

"Stage magic plays with perception." Dawkins shrugged. "At least according to this Glass character."

Lining the first aisle were glass display cases packed with top hats and wands, crystal balls and decks of playing cards; handcuffs, chains, ropes, and jewel-encrusted swords. Between were wooden boxes with hidden compartments, a telephone booth–sized chrome cage, coffins with padlocks around the lids, and a glass box filled with water and an upside-down dummy. Old-fashioned illustrated posters for Carter the Great and Mandrake the Magician and tons of people I'd never heard of hung on the walls.

Sammy knew them all. "That water torture cell back there? That's Houdini's! Do you guys have any idea how much this stuff is *worth*?"

"I don't care," Dawkins muttered. "We're racing against the clock. The next aisle is where we should find the Damascene 'Scope. Glass likely thinks it's just some sort of shoddy telescope."

"What is this competition, anyway?" Greta asked. "I thought we were supposed to be taking tests."

"The application wasn't entirely clear, Greta," Dawkins whispered, glancing back to make sure we were alone. "Tests of physical fitness were mentioned, yes, but I figured those were just, you know, to make sure that you all did well in PE."

"You couldn't have mentioned any of that on the way here?" I said.

"I didn't think it mattered," Dawkins said. "Look, this competition is just an excuse. It doesn't matter at all how you three perform."

"It matters to *me*," Greta said.

"But it's just a—" Dawkins started to say.

"It's not *just* an anything, Jack," Greta said. "It's about honor. We signed up for this thing, so we should do our best."

"I would expect no less from you, Greta," Dawkins said. "Nonetheless, that is not our mission. We are here to find the 'Scope."

We'd reached the far end of the room, and Dawkins led us around to the second aisle. Along one side were shelves of antique cameras and old movie projectors, piles of silvery metal-etched photographs, and lanterns with colored glass panes. In a row down the other side were telescopes of all kinds and sizes. At our end they were enormous, so big that they almost reached the ceiling two stories over our heads. But they got smaller as we went along, until at the other end were microscopes and spyglasses and tiny little glass things I couldn't identify.

"How big is this 'Scope?" I asked.

"I've never actually *seen* it, but I have read descriptions. It is portable, so not an enormous thing. There are two key components: First, the Damascene 'Scope proper—basically a fat tube in which special lenses are arranged. Second is a contraption called a mirror box, an arrangement of light-focusing aids like the reflector behind the bulb in a flashlight. When they are used together . . . something happens."

"'Something happens'?" Greta repeated. "What does that mean?"

"The source materials aren't entirely clear, I'm afraid. There's a lot of fancy-pants Latin—*lux chirotheca* and so on, which means 'hands of light,' though what that has to do with anything, no one says. I suspect it's some kind of dreamy description of the process when the device is activated."

"So the 'Scope is just a big metal tube?" Sammy asked.

"Yes, probably brass," Dawkins said. "The texts refer to its 'honeyed hue.'" He took out his yellow notebook and showed us a page at the back, where he'd written notes about the Damascene 'Scope—its dimensions, notations with arrows marked "VG1" through "VG3," and a shaded drawing of a sectioned tube. One end of it bristled with dials and knobs. Fixed to the top of it was another thin tube like a rifle sight.

There were at least fifteen similar-looking contraptions in this aisle alone, and though Dawkins examined each—a sailor's spyglass on a shiny tripod, a yard-long pipelike thing set in a bunch of giant gears, and more—each time he shook his head. "Apparently it's not on display."

We'd almost reached the end of the aisle where we'd started.

"What should we do now?" Greta asked.

"You should *leave* the museum this instant!" someone shouted.

Standing in the open doorway to the entry hall, his hands on his hips and a look of fury on his face, was Nestor. The white-haired little girl named Blue peeked around his back.

"How did you four get in here?" Nestor demanded.

"The door was unlocked!" Dawkins said, turning an imaginary door handle. "We bumped it, it swung open, and then we couldn't stop ourselves. Curiosity!"

"Curiosity can get you killed," Nestor said. "But never mind. Just leave. Immediately."

"Yes, sir," Dawkins said. "Why don't I go and give the truck another try, see if it's any different now that the engine's cooled."

"Get *out*," Nestor said.

We hurried past him into the entry hall, and then followed Dawkins out the front door.

Dawkins raised the hood of the truck and tinkered while I sat behind the wheel and turned the ignition key.

Even though the sun had set, the sky overhead was still deep blue with the last bit of afternoon. But you wouldn't know it near the black gloom of the house. It sucked the light right out of the air and threw the truck into shadow. Not even the glow of lights in the windows warmed up the darkness.

"That should do it," Dawkins whispered, pocketing something. "This truck isn't going anywhere."

"Let's go check KoalaKlub," Greta said.

"We will once we get some privacy." Dawkins glanced back at the dark windows of the house, where Nestor's pale face peered out. "Everyone, let's give our Mr. Nestor a warm hello."

We all turned and waved, and Nestor disappeared.

"Now that *he's* gone," Dawkins said, "why don't we take a wander 'round, see why it is they don't want us poking about."

A stone pathway led around to the back of the house.

"Another ginormous lawn," I said. Way off in the distance was a long, low building with roll-down doors. "Maybe that's what they don't want us to see?"

"Or maybe what they're hiding is in that greenhouse over there," Greta said, pointing to our right.

Though calling it a greenhouse didn't make much sense. As we got closer, I saw there were no pots, plants, bags of soil, or anything else like that. Instead, it was just an empty glass building about as big as a one-car garage attached to the back of the main house. Three walls and the roof were made of ripply panes of glass, and the floor was tiled in a weird sort of pattern—an X in a circle, like crosshairs.

"Who builds a greenhouse without plants?" Dawkins asked.

"And why stick it on the back of the museum?" Sammy said, tapping the glass to indicate a pair of closed doors. "Do plants have something to do with perceptual inquiry?"

"Maybe it was here before the museum," Greta said. "The path keeps going, all the way around the house." At the far corner up ahead, a glowing yellow rectangle was cast across the grass—light from a doorway.

"You three see where that door goes. I'll catch up to you in a moment." Dawkins pried at the panes of glass. "I want to see if we can get back into the museum through this greenhouse."

"Why are we even here?" I grumbled after Dawkins was far enough behind us not to hear. "We need to be going after the Blood Guard and stopping them from heading into a trap."

"We're doing that," Sammy said. "KoalaKlub will work. It just takes time. We'll check again after dinner."

"Right," I said. "A dead website. How can we trust that will work? How are we even going to get a safe Internet connection here?"

"Easy," Sammy said, sweeping his hand through air. "We set up a virtual private network, and we use that to encrypt everything coming or going from our computer, and then—"

From behind us came an explosion of barking—what sounded like a dozen dogs yipping and snarling.

I jumped and looked over my shoulder, expecting to see a bunch of hounds running toward us, but there wasn't anything. Just empty grass.

The snarling lowered in pitch, like the invisible dogs had something in their mouths blocking the sound. And with it, another noise: someone shrieking out—in pain?

"Where are they?" Sammy asked.

"Behind the greenhouse," I said.

"Jack!" Greta said, breaking into a run. "Hurry!"

And wishing I had a sword—or any kind of weapon at all—I ran after her.

CHAPTER 7

THE FOUR HORSEMEN—ER, *DOGS*—OF THE APOCALYPSE

We ran straight into four snarling Dobermans. They were noisy blurs of black and brown, their eyes barely visible as they dragged a bundle of rags back and forth across the grass.

I looked again.

It wasn't a bunch of rags. It was Dawkins.

One of the dogs latched on to his neck, and Greta raised her hand to smack it away.

I caught her arm and pulled her back. "Wait!" I said.

"We have to help!" Greta said, yanking herself free.

"And have the dogs bite you instead of him?"

Dawkins and the dog rolled away, his arms wrapped around it in a tight hug, while the other three dogs tugged on his legs.

Then Nestor stomped past and yanked one of the dogs away by its collar. "War!" he shouted. "Down!" He flung the dog behind him as though it weighed nothing. Nestor was a lot stronger than he looked. "Famine! Pestilence! Debra! Down! Down!"

Immediately, the other three dogs released Dawkins and edged backward, wagging their stubby tails.

Dawkins rolled over, a big smile on his face. "Since when is the fourth horseman of the apocalypse named Debra?"

"Ms. Glass felt *Death* was an inappropriate name for a female dog," Nestor said. "Are you hurt? They would not have attacked unless you were trespassing."

"Me, trespass?" Dawkins pretended to dust himself off and stood. "Ha! No, we were just playing, the dogs and me. Growls of fun can sound an awful lot like the real thing to the untrained ear."

Nestor glanced at the greenhouse, then back at Dawkins. "Do not play with these dogs. They are not pets."

"Yes, sir," Dawkins said.

"We have a mechanic coming out in the morning to inspect your vehicle. Until then, we've made up a room for you with the students on the second floor."

"Thank you," Dawkins said. "I appreciate your help."

"Don't thank *me*," Nestor said, snapping his fingers so that the four dogs came to attention. "I wanted to have you and that wreck of yours towed out of here. But Ms. Glass instructed otherwise."

"I'll thank her, then," Dawkins said. "Will she be joining us for dinner?"

Nestor turned. "Come along." The Dobermans followed him back down the path and around the corner of the house. Just before they all vanished, Nestor glanced back.

"Nestor *really* doesn't like you," Sammy said.

"Trust that the feeling is mutual," Dawkins said.

Greta hugged him. "Are you okay?"

"Sure," he said. He pulled back his left sleeve and wiped a smear of blood off his forearm: new pink skin was already filling in the gashes and tooth marks left by the dogs. "They weren't just playing," he said. "At least, not at first. That all changed once they got to know me a bit."

"But I don't understand," I said. "Why'd they attack you in the first place?"

"They didn't want me entering that greenhouse," Dawkins said. I looked over at it. Night was falling fast, and the glass box seemed full of shadow.

"But there's nothing in it," Sammy said.

"You see that and I see that," Dawkins said, "and yet those dogs are trained to attack anyone who tries to get in. Why?"

Once we were back in the house, Nestor directed us up the sweeping staircase from the entrance hall.

The upstairs looked like something out of a fancy hotel—plush red carpet, dark wood walls, everything hushed and quiet. There were four doors on each side of the hallway, and each had a nameplate. The first on the right read EVELYN TRUELOVE.

"While you were wandering around in the museum, the other students were choosing their rooms. I've marked those for your use." He glanced at his watch. "You have a few hours to make yourselves comfortable and to grab a sandwich from the dining room, before you're locked into your rooms at nine p.m."

"You lock us in our rooms?" Sammy said.

"It's not that we don't trust you," Nestor said, the smile on his face saying he didn't trust us at all, "but more for safety's sake. And because we want our contestants to have a full night's rest."

Dawkins pushed open the door and steered us into my room. Like the hallway, it was all dark wood and satin wall hangings, along with a big old desk that made even the gigantic bed look small. An interior door connected the room to the next one in the hall, but when I turned the handle, I found it was locked.

"Stop fussing about, Ronan," Dawkins said, pulling the laptop from his bag. "We need to check out KoalaKlub post-haste and see if anyone's stopped by and left a message."

Sammy sat at the desk, pulled the laptop in front of him, and powered it up. "Nestor gave me the wifi password. Shouldn't take long to set up our own secure private network."

While he bent over the keyboard and started typing, Dawkins took out the orange emergency cell phone and cycled through the screens. "No messages, no calls."

And there was no change at all in KoalaLou's treehouse.

"Should we be worried?" Greta asked Dawkins.

"We should be worried," I said.

"No," Dawkins said, biting his lip. "Maybe. I can't really say." He stared at the image on the laptop. "I won't lie: I don't like that we haven't heard from anyone yet. But it hasn't even been a day. They're likely still on the road, or sitting down to dinner. Speaking of which . . ."

Sammy typed something and the screen saver kicked on. "Now only someone who knows the password can access it."

"And what's the password?" I asked.

"The name of the person we're here to save," Sammy said, and I thought of Flavia's locket around my mom's neck, the pictures inside of the black-haired little boy and girl. "No one else is going to know that. And we're not going to forget it."

Ms. Glass didn't join us for our sandwich dinner, in person or in robot.

The robot *was* there, but it wasn't Ms. Glass this time around. Instead it silently acted as a waiter, rolling through the swinging doors into the kitchen, and then returning moments later with a silver tray loaded down with sandwiches and drinks.

So it was just the seven of us in the high-ceilinged dining room. The dark wooden table was probably long enough to seat forty, but we huddled at one end of it, while Blue, Elspeth, and Kieran ate at the other end. Oil portraits looked down on us from the walls.

"I wonder who those guys are," I said.

"Magicians," Sammy said around a mouthful of ham and cheese. "That one there is Howard Thurston, and next to him is Pendark the Great."

"How do you know all this stuff?" I asked him.

"There weren't always video games at the fosters, so I'd get books from the library." He shrugged. "I like magic."

"You're gonna need some magic to win tomorrow," Kieran called from the other end of the table.

"Why are you so snotty?" Greta asked. "We're taking tests, not dueling to the death."

The little girl Blue said, "Actually, the tests kind of *are* duels. Not to the death, but, like, you know what I mean, right?"

"No," Greta said. "We *don't* know. That's why I'm asking."

Blue picked up her sandwich. It looked huge in her hands. "Then I guess you'll find out tomorrow morning."

"Jack," Greta whispered, "what have you gotten us into?"

"You'll be fine," Dawkins whispered back. "Our foes are not the mouthy kids at the other end of the table. Don't forget why we're here." He didn't have to say the rest: *These people have something we can use to save Flavia and the world.* "Nothing else matters."

After dinner, Sammy did a quick check of KoalaKlub, but there were still no responses to our message. Greta was as worried as I was about what sort of trap our parents might be heading into, but as Sammy said, "There's not a whole lot more we can do tonight, guys."

Dawkins yawned. "Sammy has the right of it. Things will look different in the morning."

We all went to our separate rooms. Mine, Sammy's, and Greta's were all in a row—Greta quickly unlocked the connecting doors between. "Can never play it too safe," she said as she came in.

Dawkins' room, however, was across the hall. There was no easy way to unlock his door without our getting caught, so we left him alone.

"Nestor was right: we should get some rest," Greta said, going back to her room. "Night before the big test and all that."

Only, I couldn't sleep.

It wasn't that I was worried about tomorrow's test. Dawkins was right: the tests didn't matter. I was worried about my mom. She was in danger again, and she didn't even know it. Worse, my dad knew she was coming, and he had the upper hand this time. There was no way I could stop him.

Or was there?

I went to the laptop and typed in the password—"Flavia." But instead of visiting KoalaKlub, I opened a new window and logged on to the ILZ gamer board for the first time in months. There were a bunch of old emails in my inbox (I never delete anything), but it was the most

82

recent conversation I was interested in—the one where my mom had pretended to be me.

Dad's handle was Sisyphus79, after that guy who never manages to roll his big rock to the top of the hill. Mine was DorkLord2K1.

From: Sisyphus79
To: DorkLord2K1
Ronan,
I sometimes worry that you aren't actually reading what I write to you. Am I getting through? [He definitely knew he was writing to my mom.]
You have been told that the Blood Guard is all good, and that the Bend Sinister is all bad, but that is not true. The Bend is engaged in a noble project to better all of mankind, and the terrible things you've seen are merely the ugly means to an end that will benefit everyone in the world.

He went on like that for a while, but I skipped to the last paragraph.

I am thrilled that you've agreed to take a chance and meet with me. I give you my word that I will come alone and unarmed. You can trust me, Ronan, as I have always trusted you.

Liar, I thought. *If you trust me so much, why'd you hide a tracking device in my baseball?*

The next email was from my mom, pretending to be me.

From: DorkLord2K1
To: Sisyphus79
Okay. You promise to come alone and I promise to let you explain everything. It's a deal. If I can get away tomorrow morning, I should be able to reach Minneapolis by Sunday night. See you soon. R

I realized I was holding my head in my hands. The email didn't sound like me at all. No way it would have fooled my dad. It was way too formal. I would have ended the email with a simple "CU" instead of writing out "See you soon" and then adding my initial. Who writes that way?

Parents.

There was one more email—an unopened one that had come from my dad only an hour ago. After my mom and the Blood Guard had gone after him, after we'd escaped Patch Steiner. The subject line was "Olive Branch."

From: Sisyphus79
To: DorkLord2K1
Ronan,
I hope this note reaches the real you.
You have escaped my agent, so you've likely figured out that the Blood Guard is off on a fool's errand. In trying to deceive me, they've deceived themselves. I will capture your mother and her friends, and I will use them to demonstrate why I and the Bend Sinister are not to be toyed with.
Or you can save them.

84

Tell me where you are, and we can have a meeting, father to son, man to man. No Blood Guard, no Bend Sinister, just two people who care about each other.

In return, I give you my word I will not to subject your mother or her friends to any unnecessary pain.

It's on you, son.

But don't think it over for too long. Let me know before my "meeting" with your mother early Sunday evening. Otherwise, I will begin thinning the ranks of the Blood Guard, starting with someone you care deeply about. Want to guess who?

Tick tock, Ronan.

I scrambled backward—away from the email, away from the desk, the chair falling over behind me.

I had to tell Dawkins.

In a panic, I ran to the door and yanked on the knob.

It wouldn't turn.

Right. We were locked in at night. I could go wake up Sammy and Greta, but what would they be able to do?

Instead, I made myself take five slow, deep breaths, and reminded myself that my dad had no idea where I was, that I didn't need to freak out just because of an email.

It's on you.

I went back to the desk and rolled the cursor over the REPLY button. And I thought hard.

I would give myself over to him—not happily, but I'd do it—if that would save my mom and the rest of the Blood Guard and get Flavia's soul back. But would he actually keep his word? Would he honor the deal he was offering? Or would he just go on lying to me as he'd been doing all my life?

I reread the emails. I had until Sunday night. Two nights from now. More than enough time for the Blood Guard to find Dawkins' message in KoalaKlub, more than enough time for them to avoid my dad's trap.

And if KoalaKlub *didn't* work—well, at least I knew how to stop my dad before anyone got hurt.

I logged out and closed the laptop, and even though I thought I'd never fall asleep, the next thing I knew, the room was bright with morning light, my door was being thrown open, and Nestor was announcing that it was "Time to face the Gauntlet!"

But I barely listened, because in the hall behind Nestor, Greta was shouting about something. "What do you mean? Where? When?"

"When what?" I asked, sitting up.

"Dawkins," Greta said to me. "He's disappeared!"

CHAPTER 8
WHAT WOULD DAWKINS DO?

"But *how* can he be gone?" I asked Nestor, grabbing his coat sleeve.

"Quite easily," Nestor said, staring down at my fingers until I let go. "We allowed him to sleep here, yes, but only until a mechanic could fix that wreck of his. He departed early this morning."

"It doesn't even look like he slept in his bed," I said, pointing into the empty room.

"The housekeeper tidied up," Nestor said. "Listen, it is 8:03. You children do not have time to endlessly debate the whereabouts of your . . . whatever he was. You need to dress, eat breakfast, and be ready for the first test at nine a.m. sharp."

Elspeth, Kieran, and Blue leaned out into the hallway to see what was going on, but then pulled their heads back and shut their doors.

Nestor curled up the corners of his mouth so that his teeth showed—he was trying to smile, I realized—and then went down the stairs.

"*Nice* guy," Sammy said.

"Did you notice how he talked about Jack in the past tense?" Greta asked. "'Whatever he *was*.' It's like he thinks Jack no longer exists."

"It's obvious he's lying," I said, walking back into my room. "A mechanic would have seen immediately that there was nothing wrong with the truck."

"Something terrible's happened, I just know it." Greta closed the door.

"We need to check KoalaKlub," Sammy said, following me inside.

In KoalaLou's treehouse, we found a new message chalked in orange beneath our earlier note.

WILL CALL FOR MEET—O

"Ogabe?" I asked.

"Know any other O's?" Sammy said, sitting back and staring at the screen. "So maybe Ogabe called Jack, and maybe Jack went to meet him?"

"And maybe, because it was the middle of the night . . . ," I said.

"Jack . . . didn't want to wake us up?" Sammy said, frowning. "Maybe he thought he'd be back by now?"

"Too many maybes," Greta said. "He wouldn't go without leaving a note. That's not like Jack."

"We don't know for certain that he's in trouble," I said.

"He might have just gone off to meet Ogabe. But just to be safe, let's tell Ogabe Jack's gone." I walked KoalaLou over to the box of chalk and took out a blue stick.

JACK GONE. WITH YOU? WE ARE AT GLASS ESTATE.—RGS

"We can check it later," I said. "Right now, we need to focus. Our mission is to sit for this Glass Gauntlet, right? So let's do that: sharpen up our pencils or whatever and take this test."

"*Ace* this test, you mean," Greta said. "I intend to win."

But we had it all wrong: the test had nothing to do with papers and pencils.

When we arrived downstairs, we found Blue and Elspeth waiting in the entrance hall.

"What's with the church clothes?" Elspeth asked. She had her long dark hair braided tight against her skull and was dressed in tight-fitting workout clothes like my mom might wear. Beside her, Blue was in holey jeans and a yellow T-shirt. Kieran was nowhere to be seen.

I looked down at my khakis, white button-down, and blazer, just like the ones Greta and Sammy wore. On our way through DC, we had stopped at a mall to buy appropriate test-taking clothes. Elspeth was right, we looked like we were in a Sunday school uniform. "Um, dress for success?"

I took my coat off and left it on a chair, and Sammy and Greta did the same.

Elspeth snorted and said, "I'll be so glad when you idiots are cut from the competition."

The front door opened, and Nestor and a tall blond woman stood in the entryway.

"Hello, children!" she said. "I am Vaughn, and I am the official proctor for the Glass Gauntlet. We have arranged transportation outside. Please follow me, and we will get started."

"Kieran's not here," Blue said as we all stepped out onto the porch.

"Who?" Vaughn asked.

"The boy with the spiky hair," Blue said.

"We can't be responsible for every vain, tardy child," Vaughn said. "If he can't be here on time, he will be the first student cut from the competition."

The two golf carts were waiting on the front drive. Vaughn got behind the wheel of one, and Nestor took the second. "Get in, get in," she said. "We are on a schedule."

Elspeth slid onto the back of Vaughn's cart, so Greta, Sammy, and I climbed into the second behind Nestor. Blue looked back and forth between the two carts, trying to decide which to take, I guess, when all of sudden the front door was flung open again, and Kieran bolted out.

"I'm here!" he shouted. "Don't leave without me!"

Maybe he *had* been messing with his hair, because it looked freshly spiked. He was clutching an iPad in one hand, and something had happened to the bottom half of his face—a giant grin of blood-flecked, fanglike teeth

90

stretched from ear to ear. He looked terrifying, like some kind of murderous, undead zombie clown.

"His face!" Sammy whispered, edging closer to me.

"It's okay," I said, squinting at it. "He's just wearing a mask." It was a realistic paint job, but now I could see the metal bars over the mouth hole, and how the whole thing strapped around the back of his head.

"It just reminds me of . . ." Sammy didn't finish, but he didn't have to—he was thinking of the Bend Sinister mask my dad wore when he'd almost killed Sammy.

"He's just trying to psych us out," Greta said. "Don't let him get to you."

Blue hopped into the front beside Nestor. "Isn't this exciting?" she said, turning sideways.

Nestor gave the cart some juice, and we turned a tight loop, heading not down the driveway, but instead along one of the stone pathways and out across the grass. After a few turns, the black house disappeared from view behind us.

"I'd be more excited if I knew where we were going," Greta said. "We don't really know a lot about these tests."

Nestor chuckled and said, "Oh, you'll find out very shortly now, Ms. Sustermann."

That wasn't very reassuring.

"What does Kieran have on his face?" I asked.

"That's just his bite guard," Blue said. "He used to have to wear it at the orphanage so that he wouldn't bite the other kids. Now he just wears it because it likes it."

"He's a biter?" I said. "Great. That's just great."

"Where's that old guy who came with you?" Blue asked. Her eyes never left us. It was creepy in a little kid sort of way.

"They fixed his truck and made him leave," Greta said. "Parents aren't supposed to hang around."

Beside Blue, Nestor made a little *hmmph* sound.

"That's the rule!" Blue said. "But he's *not* your parent, right? What is he to you?"

What a strange question. Blue looked like a nine-year-old, but she was clearly super smart or she wouldn't have been there. Someone thought that she could take on that Elspeth girl and bite-mask boy and win.

Greta squinted at her, looking as suspicious as I felt. "He's our *friend*."

"If you say so," Blue said, "but what kind of friend takes off without saying good-bye?"

We came over a low rise and the two carts pulled to a stop.

"Behold the famous Glass hedge maze!" Vaughn announced.

"Behold?" Greta whispered to me and Sammy. "Really?"

"Is it famous because it's so creepy looking?" Sammy asked.

Sammy was right—the hedge maze looked like some kind of witch's playground, a solid brown wall of dead bushes a couple of football fields long and a dozen feet high. They'd been neatly trimmed, and they still had enough shriveled yellowed leaves so that it was impossible to see through them, but mostly they looked like . . . thorny sticks.

"At the heart of the maze," Vaughn continued, "is an item of great value. The person who retrieves it will be named the winner of this heat of the Glass Gauntlet. The next four competitors will find numbered envelopes with the keys to round two. But for the final person who reaches the maze's center, there will be only our thanks for having taken part."

"What are the rules?" Greta asked.

Vaughn didn't answer. "We will drop each of you at one of six designated starting points. Wait there until—" She motioned to Nestor and he squeezed a button on an air horn. The blare was loud enough to make me cover my ears. "That is the signal for you to begin."

The two carts went in opposite directions, ours along the stone pathway until we reached a black disk set in the grass like a granite manhole cover about forty feet away from the hedge maze.

"Samuel Warner," Nestor said.

Looking confused, Sammy got out and walked over to the disk. "Here?"

But Nestor just stomped on the gas. We shot off down the curved path another hundred yards. "Blue!" he barked, and the little blond girl got out. Another hundred yards and he announced, "Greta Sustermann!"

Finally it was my turn.

To the right of my starting mark I could see Greta waving, and an equal distance beyond her, Blue hopping

93

from foot to foot. To my left was Kieran. He didn't look up, too busy messing around with his iPad.

What I couldn't see in any direction was an opening in the hedge wall. We were supposed to run a maze like lab rats, I got that. But how was I supposed to get in? Run around the outside until I found the entrance?

And then Nestor blasted the air horn and the hedges in front of me crackled apart like a set of wicker curtains, creating a space just wide enough for a person to pass through. I looked right and saw Greta dashing toward a similar opening. So each of us got our own entrance.

Kieran strolled forward, eyes on the slim device in his hand.

I took off running.

The walls were already ratcheting closed again. I wasn't going to make it. So I dove forward.

And barely cleared the hedges, the thorny branches scratching my face and snagging the cuff of my shirt. I landed in a heap on a dirty tiled path.

Behind me, the hedges shuddered together.

I was in an aisle formed by two walls of dead bushes. I got down on my knees to see if I could crawl under them, but it turned out the hedges were set in individual metal planters slotted into metal rails. I figured that must be how they moved around. Probably why they'd died, too—hard to have a healthy root system in a skinny little pot.

To my left, where Kieran had gone, the aisle dead-ended, so I went the other way.

I rounded the corner and found an open passage in front of me: I could see clear past layer after layer of dead shrubbery, a sunny, straight pathway all the way to the center of the maze. There, a low, grassy hill rose up to a stumpy little tree and a stone pedestal at its summit.

It couldn't be this easy, could it?

I sprinted as hard as I could toward the hill but had only taken fifteen steps when a wall of spiny brush zoomed in from the right and cut me off.

I bounced off of it and fell backward, then reached up to touch my cheek. My fingers came away wet with blood. This "test" was going to kill us if we weren't careful. What had Dawkins gotten us into?

Around me, the walls of the maze noisily reformed every other minute. As I got back to my feet, the ends of the aisle I was in actually closed themselves off, so that I was caught in the middle of a hedge box. "Come on!" I shouted at the sky. "How is this even fair?"

And then a face appeared against the bright blue: Greta. She was on top, looking down at me. Her nice new button-down was torn and bloody, too, even worse than mine. But she was grinning. "Give up already, Truelove?"

"What are you doing up there?" I said.

"This test is completely bogus," she said. "But I figure if the maze won't play nice, then we shouldn't either."

"But isn't that cheating?" I asked.

"They never said we had to stay *in* the maze, Ronan.

And I am not going to lose to that horrible Elspeth girl."
She reached down. "Need a hand up?"

I shoved my hands into the hedge and grabbed fistfuls of branches—something jabbed my palms, but I ignored it. "Nah, go ahead. I can get up on my own."

"Careful up here. The footing is tricky!" She saluted me, said, "See you at the finish line," and then vanished.

The hedge I was climbing started moving when I was halfway up, so I just hung on until it stopped fifty feet and a ninety-degree turn closer to the center. By the time I got to the top, my hands were scratched all over, too, like Greta's.

She had almost reached the center. I watched as she rode one moving hedge like a surfer atop a surfboard, and then carefully stepped onto another when it passed close by.

From up here it was kind of mesmerizing, the way the walls moved, snaking around, forming dead ends and loops and zigzags.

All, that is, except to my left, where they pulled apart one after another, forming a straight line from the outside to the center.

Kieran. Somehow he was using his iPad to rewrite the maze.

Cheater, I thought—but then I corrected myself. Greta was right: We hadn't been given any rules. Hijacking the maze was just as fair as running on top of it.

But no way was I going to let him win.

The hedge top was like a lumpy, thorny sidewalk—

almost but not quite flat enough for running. I had to jog in a weird crouch, which was bad enough. Worse was when the hedges *moved*. I put my foot down and the hedge shot out from under me, so that I tumbled over and almost rolled to the ground. But then I was up again and moving fast, straight for Kieran.

Greta had made it to the center of the maze and was climbing down.

Unfortunately, I wasn't the only one who'd spotted her.

With a roar, Kieran dropped his iPad and bolted forward. He wasn't worried about getting stuck on the bushes, so he moved tons faster than Greta—fast enough that I knew he was going to catch her.

I didn't give a monkey's butt about this stupid test, but I *did* care about Greta.

I sprinted—ignoring how my feet kept twisting in the twiggy top of the hedgerow—and leaped to the ground behind him. But too late: there was no way I'd be able to stop him.

What would Dawkins do? I wondered.

"Look out!" I screamed. "It's behind you!"

Kieran glanced back, slowing down just long enough for me to throw myself forward.

He stepped aside.

And I shot right past and hit the ground.

Kieran snickered and turned back to Greta again, but I was close enough now. I reached out, grabbed his ankle, and held tight.

He fell on top of me, grabbed my head with both hands, and brought that terrifying mask down toward my face. All I could see were his giant bloody fangs, all I could feel was his hot breath, all I could hear were his teeth snapping together behind the mask.

CHAPTER 9

STICKING OUT LIKE
A GLASS THUMB

"**G**et off him!" someone shouted.

And then Kieran was gone, knocked aside by something small and fast.

Sammy.

The two of them rolled away on the grass. Sammy got up holding his shoulder. "Tackles *hurt*. How do football players do that?"

"They wear pads." I got up and backed away from Kieran. "That was really not cool, dude."

Breathing heavily, Kieran looked from me to Sammy and back again, then up the grassy hill toward the tree. "You let her win!"

I shrugged. "Somebody had to."

"Idiots!" he shouted, and then he took off straight for the tree, where Greta stood holding something boxy in her hands.

She ducked away as Kieran ran toward her, but he wasn't interested in her anymore; he was after the envelopes on the pedestal beside the tree. He grabbed one and moved off to open it and read the message inside.

"We should probably get those other envelopes," I said. "So that we don't get kicked out."

Just before we reached the tree, something small and pale dashed between us: that Blue girl. She snatched one of the envelopes and held it over her head. "I'm in!" she shouted.

At that moment, Elspeth burst out of the maze a hundred feet to our right. "I can't have lost," she said. "No way am I last."

Sammy and I each picked one of the remaining two envelopes and waved them at her.

Elspeth turned on Greta, her eyes angry slits. "I saw you *on top* of the maze—that's cheating!"

"It's fair and you know it," Kieran muttered. "Anything goes in the Glass Gauntlet."

Sammy, Greta, and I moved away from the others, into the shade of the tree, where a leaky coil of hose as fat around as a firehose had muddied the grass.

"You'd think someone would water those poor bushes," Greta said.

"Too late for that," I said, and opened my envelope. The only thing inside was a message reading "Congratulations! You have moved on to the next challenge." Sammy's said the same thing.

"Greta, what was in your envelope?" I asked.

"It wasn't an envelope. It was a box." She showed us a wooden chest the size of a cigar box. Inside was what looked like a segmented, transparent tube.

"What the heck is that?" Sammy asked.

I lifted it out. It was formed from a kind of hardened glass, with ultra-thin brass wires running through the transparent material. The narrowest part tapered to a point, while the bigger part was about as big as the ball of my thumb. In fact, that's sort of what it looked like. Suddenly I knew. "It's the thumb section," I said. "Of the Glass Gauntlet."

"But that's just the name of the test," Greta said. "It's not an actual thing . . . is it?"

I slipped the glass thumb over my own; it fit almost perfectly. "Looks like it."

"What's it do?" Sammy asked.

"Not much." I bent it back and forth a few times. "Maybe we need the rest of it."

"You know what this means?" Greta asked, grinning. "Now I have to win *all* the challenges."

I laughed and replaced the glass thumb in the box, and Greta closed the lid.

The air horn sounded again, the maze walls pulled apart, and the two carts rolled up to the foot of the hill.

"Congratulations!" Vaughn said to Greta. "And well done to the rest of you. You've each managed to get through the maze in your own, clever ways."

"She cheated," Elspeth said, pointing at Greta. "She went on *top* of the maze. Running a maze doesn't mean running *over* it."

Vaughn tsk-tsked. "You know the rules, Ms. Carnahan—there are no rules. The Glass Gauntlet tests problem-solving skills. And on this test, Miss Sustermann was the winner. Now please, we will return to the house for lunch and a rest period. The second test commences at two o'clock."

As we walked down the hill to the carts, Kieran said, "You're lucky I was wearing this protective mask, Truelove. Or else you wouldn't have a nose anymore."

"Is that a threat?" I asked.

"It's a fact," he said. "I wear this"—he flicked a nail against the painted plastic on his face—"to protect my opponents. Because I'm a ferocious *animal*, man. No telling what I might do when I'm all riled up."

"This is only a test," I said. "Why would you bite someone's nose off just for a dumb test?"

"Because of the money, duh," he said. "A million bucks. I'd be set for life."

Nobody needs money that badly, I thought. "How did you get through so fast?" I asked to change the subject.

"Hacked the program off Nestor's desktop. His lock screen doesn't come up right away, so when he went out front this morning with Vaughn, I sneaked in and mirrored the remote program to my iPad." His shoulders slumped, and he looked back at the maze. "Oh, man—I dropped it in there."

"You didn't think that was cheating?" I asked.

"Cheating's the whole *point* of the Gauntlet," he replied. "Gotta go find my iPad."

Blue climbed into our cart. "That was awesome how you ran on top of the maze."

"I got lucky," Greta said. "If Ronan hadn't tackled Kieran, I wouldn't have made it."

Blue's eyes turned to me. "Why didn't you let him fight her? You could have won."

That had never even occurred to me. I didn't care whether I won or not, but Greta *did*. "She's my friend," I told Blue. "I didn't want her to get hurt."

"Dumb," Blue replied, shaking her head.

Lunch wasn't much: just grilled ham and cheese sandwiches, chips, and a big basket of oranges. We ate on a patio off the kitchen, the three of us by ourselves at a table on one side and Blue and Kieran at a table on the other. We watched in silence as Vaughn drove Elspeth away on one of the golf carts.

"One down, four to go," Greta said.

We were served by the robot again. "Weird how sometimes it doesn't talk," I said.

"I think different people operate it at different times," Sammy said.

"So it's not always Ms. Glass," Greta said. "Right now it could be—whoever—the cook."

"Right." Sammy glanced over at Kieran and Blue, then whispered, "I picked this up in the maze." He slid Kieran's iPad from under his shirt.

"Sammy!" Greta hissed. "That's stealing!"

"If there are no rules in these tests," I said, "then there's no rule about borrowing each other's stuff."

"I stopped caring whether I'm nice to him after he tried to bite off Ronan's nose," Sammy said, tucking it back under his shirt. "I'll give him back his iPad after we're all done."

At the other table, Blue was plowing through a stack of oranges, peeling them fast and stuffing wedges into her mouth. Watching her pig out made me think of Dawkins. Where had he gone? And why he hadn't taken us with him?

"It's not nice to stare," Blue called out. "I like oranges. That bother you?"

"Sorry," I said. "I was just thinking about our friend Jack."

"The guy who ran away in the middle of the night?" she asked.

"He didn't run away," I said and turned my chair back. Strange kid.

Greta opened the wooden box again, took out the glass thumb section, and bent it back and forth at the joints. "These filaments look like they go to these contacts here at the base."

"Probably connects to the other sections of the hand," Sammy said. "Maybe this is part of some old magic trick."

"Or maybe," I said softly, thinking aloud, "it's related to the 'Scope. What did Dawkins say about that Latin phrase. . .?"

"'Hands of light,'" Greta murmured.

"Maybe that's this thing," I said.

"But these are fingers of glass," Sammy said. "Unless there's some kind of magic to it we can't see."

I glanced back to make sure no one was close by, then used my pinky to hook the chain around my neck and pull my Verity Glass out from under my shirt. I couldn't touch the purplish disk without thinking of my mom, remembering how she gave it to me and told me to keep it secret. As I turned over in my hand, I wondered where she was and whether she was okay. "We need to check KoalaKlub again."

Then I turned my attention to the glass thumb. Dawkins had told me the Verity Glass had many properties, and I'd even seen a few of them myself—how it could reveal the true natures of the Pure, the Blood Guard, and the Bend Sinister. Maybe it could reveal something special about this strange Gauntlet thing.

I peered through the Verity Glass. There was a little shimmer of light along the brass wires of the thumb, but nothing else.

"See anything?" Sammy asked.

"Nope," I said.

"What's that?" Blue asked. Suddenly she was right there next to me, threads of orange peel stuck to her lips.

"*Ah!*" I said, startled, dropping the Verity Glass on its chain. It swung down and knocked against my chest. My breath caught in my throat. How could I be so stupid, playing around with it in front of strangers?

"It's his purple monocle," Sammy said. "He thinks it makes him look cool."

"It's kind of a family heirloom." Since I already had it out, I figured I might as well take a quick peek at everyone here to make sure they weren't Bend Sinister. Through the lens, Kieran, Sammy, and Blue looked like themselves, only a lot more violet. Greta, as usual, was a blindingly bright figure, a person who seemed to be made of light—which is how all Pure souls look through a Verity Glass.

"Can I see?" Blue asked.

No way could I let Blue look through it. Who knows what she'd say if she saw Greta.

"Sorry, but I, um, promised my mom I wouldn't let anything happen to it." I slipped it back under my shirt.

After a minute, Blue said, "Fine, be that way." She wandered back over to the other table.

Greta raised her eyebrows. "You really ought to be more careful."

"No kidding." I looked out across the lawn. As I watched, Nestor steered one of the golf carts away from the house. "There goes Nestor and the dogs."

"Then the coast is clear," Greta said. "Time to find out what happened to Jack."

CHAPTER 10
THE DAMASCENE 'SCOPE

With the sun high overhead, the empty greenhouse shimmered like a box full of light.

"Kind of hard to hide someone in a transparent building," I said, wondering why we were back here again.

"I never said he'd be in here," Greta said. "But the dogs attacked Jack when he tried to get in. Why?"

"Maybe they just attack sneaky-looking people," I said.

"Like us?" Sammy asked.

I glanced over my shoulder, but there was no sign of the Dobermans. Or of anyone. Just acres of grass, trees, and that faraway building with the roll-down doors in the distance.

"Maybe we should check out that garage," I said. "We could use one of their cars to go get help."

"From who? Everyone—your mom, my dad, Ogabe, the entire Blood Guard, even Jack—has disappeared." At the corner of the greenhouse were two skinny hinges and a tiny latch with a keyhole. Greta crouched down in front of it with a paper clip. "Make sure no one sneaks up on us."

"No one's going to sneak—" I looked up and across the empty greenhouse and yelped.

Staring at us from the other side, her face and hands flattened against the glass, was Blue.

I motioned her over. "What are you doing?"

"What are *you* doing?" she said, making her eyes bug out.

"What's it look like?" Sammy said. "We're breaking into this greenhouse."

"Taking you long enough," Blue said, tracing a circle on the glass with her finger.

"Think you can do it faster?" Greta asked.

"No," Blue said. "But I'd hurry up if I were you."

"Oh? Why's that?" I asked.

"You don't hear them?" she asked.

Greta stopped fiddling with the door and we all listened.

"All I hear is the wind blow—" Sammy started, but then stopped. "Oh no."

The dogs: their terrifying snarling, growing louder by the second.

"Greta," I said, "step it up."

"I'm trying!" she said, her ear against the lock.

Now, in addition to their growls, I could hear the jingle of metal—the noise from their chain collars.

With a rusty *thunk*, the door creaked open.

Greta fell in, Blue and Sammy almost on top of her, and then I hopped over them, slammed the door, and twisted the latch.

As I did, the four dogs tumbled around the corner, a brown and black blur. They yipped and ran right up to the glass, then took one look at us and quieted. All four sat back on their haunches and silently stared.

Somehow that was even scarier.

"Why are they looking at us like that?" Sammy asked, scrambling backward.

"They're probably hungry," Blue said.

"You're not making this better!" I was sweating, and not just because four bloodthirsty Dobermans a few inches away were patiently waiting to devour us. All that glass in the walls and ceiling focused the sunlight and made it super warm. "It feels like we're under a magnifying glass in here."

"We should get into the museum before Nestor comes to see why the dogs were barking," Greta said, pushing aside a massive old wooden tripod that was blocking the doors. "Huh," she said, turning the handle. "It's unlocked."

The doors opened onto a room that blazed so bright with light I had to cover my eyes. In front of us was an angled mirrored divider that separated the room into two chambers, but before I could see anything more, the door shut behind us and everything went pitch-black again.

I stretched my hands out until my fingers touched something cool and smooth.

"The walls feel like glass," Greta said.

"This is the mirror maze," said Blue. "There's a big sliding door in the museum hall that connects to it but it's off-limits like everything else in this place."

"I guess that explains why it got so bright in here," I said. "The reflected light from the greenhouse." Sliding my left hand along the wall, I walked forward. Pretty soon I hit the divider, and followed it around into another chamber. "We're not going to get lost, are we?"

"Nah," Blue said from directly ahead of me. "I already found the door out. Here." She guided my hands in the dark until I could feel a handle. "It's too heavy for me to move. I don't weigh enough."

With a low screech, the door rolled about three feet.

We scooted around the edge into the museum, and behind us, the door shut again with a soft, solid *whump*. We'd ended up back in the aisle with all the old telescopes and microscopes and spyglasses.

"What's that?" I said. Right by the mirror maze's door was a wheeled cart covered with a purple tarp. I yanked the cloth away. Underneath was a wooden box the size a coffin. The lid was loose, so Sammy and I lifted it away.

The stink of well-oiled metal flooded out. Loosely packed inside was a sectioned brass tube about six feet long and maybe a foot in diameter, with another, thinner tube fixed to the top like a rifle scope. One end was studded with a bunch of dials and knobs.

Etched into the brass was an inscription. I traced it with my fingertip, reading, "He came near Damascus:

and suddenly there shined round about him a light from Heaven. ACTS 9:3."

Damascus. So that's where it got its name. The Damascene 'Scope.

And then Blue was pushing in beside me. "What is it?" She ran her dirty fingers along the metal, catching her index finger on a little brass loop at one of the seamed joints between the sections.

"This thing is super old," I said, "you probably shouldn't mess—"

But she'd already yanked on it. A panel as wide around and thin as a dinner plate rotated out. A web of brass metalwork reached from its outer edge to a hole in the center about as big as a golf ball.

"Pretty," Blue said.

Greta leaned in next to us. "Look," she said, "there's one on this end, too." She tugged on another loop, and another metal framework came out. It looked exactly the same as the first, except for one difference: mounted in the center hole was a lens of violet glass that looked an awful lot like the one dangling on a chain around my neck.

A Verity Glass.

"Ronan," Sammy asked, "is that what I think it is?"

"That looks like your purple monocle," Blue said, reaching over and tapping her fingernail against the glass under my shirt. "I bet yours fits in the empty hole on this one." She put her thumb through the empty space on the first panel. "You should try it."

I wished again she hadn't seen my Verity Glass. And I knew I shouldn't listen to her, but . . . what harm could it do to see if she was right? I slipped the chain over my head, took the Verity Glass by its edges, and carefully slid it into the empty spot on the first panel.

It fit perfectly. There was even a little divot in the mounting for the place where the chain was connected to the silver frame.

"It's like that monocle was *made* for this thing," Blue said. She pulled a strand of hair forward and chewed on it.

"Maybe," I said. According to Dawkins, the core of the Damascene 'Scope was this lens array and the lenses that went inside of it. Verity Glasses?

"And there's one over here." Sammy pulled on another brass loop in the seam closest to me and exposed a third plate. Like the first, this one was empty.

I lifted my Verity Glass from the mount and quickly hung it around my neck. Then the three of us rotated the panels back into place.

"We should probably cover this up again," Sammy said, the purple tarp in his arms.

"That won't be necessary," a voice said. "I am getting *very tired* of finding you kids where you're not supposed to be."

Nestor was standing at the head of the aisle. "The collection is *valuable*, so we monitor it." He pointed and we looked up, right into the lens of a closed-circuit camera.

"*Busted*," Blue whispered.

CHAPTER 11

YOU CAN DUNK A KID IN WATER, BUT YOU CAN'T MAKE HIM SINK

"We know we shouldn't have sneaked in," Greta started to say, going into full apology mode.

But Nestor raised his palm to stop her. "I do *not* want to hear it. You children are all shameless liars and wicked cheats, and I am not going to listen to your prevarications."

"I don't even know what 'prevarications' *means*," Sammy said.

"I will consult with Ms. Glass and deal with you three after the next event," Nestor said.

Blue stepped out from between me and Greta and waved. "Don't forget about me!"

Nestor blinked. "Ah—correction, the *four* of you. Now come along, it is time for the second challenge." He walked away, his heels clicking on the tile. At the door of the museum, he turned and said, "Are you deaf? What are you waiting for? It's time for the next heat of the Glass Gauntlet!"

We stood in a row along the edge of the giant round pool. A breeze sent little ripples across the shallow water, but the waves didn't obscure the maze design in the tile at the bottom. I was relieved to hear that the pattern was only for looks; I couldn't imagine how we would *swim* a labyrinth.

Instead, we were supposed to paddle across while standing on neon-colored, round plastic floats.

"The first of you to reach the island will find a prize of inestimable value," Vaughn said. The island was a round little patio in the center of the pool, the sort of place you'd crawl out onto to sunbathe during a summer swim.

I toed the float. Two canvas straps were set into the top—to hold on to? To tuck our feet under? To slide our legs through? "How are we supposed to propel these things?" I asked.

"With one of these," Vaughn said. Beside her, Nestor held up a six-foot long plastic shaft with a paddle on each end. "You may stand or kneel or sit. We do not care. The only rule of this challenge is that you *not* fall into the water."

Greta raised her hand. "I've already won once. What happens if I get cut?"

"The prize you won will be forfeit," Vaughn said. "In the Glass Gauntlet, winner takes all."

"I guess I better win again, then," Greta said.

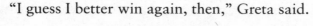

A snort came from behind us. Kieran. He was wearing his creepy bloody teeth mask again, as well as swim trunks and a shirt that looked like it was part of a scuba suit. "You three don't look very prepared."

"We don't need swimsuits," I said, kicking off my sneakers. "We've got skills."

"As before, once the horn sounds, you may begin." Vaughn pointed. "Samuel, you are at one o'clock. Kieran, two o'clock. Greta, three o'clock. Ronan, four o'clock. And Blue, five o'clock. Good luck to each of you."

Nestor waited to blow the horn until we had each plunked our float into the water and climbed aboard.

My electric purple float tipped and tilted under my feet, and for a second I thought I was going right into the water, and then . . . "*Rolleo*," I muttered.

What I'd said to Kieran about how we had skills? I wasn't lying.

On the hottest day of July, Dawkins had led us to the swimming pool beside the Wilson Peak lodge. Four fat logs floated in the water. "Welcome to the first-ever Blood Guard Rolleo!"

"You've got to be kidding," Greta said. "Do I look like a lumberjack?"

"No, but on days like this, you smell like one!" Greta swung at him, but he dodged her by stepping onto the closest log. It turned under his feet.

But instead of spilling off, he bent his legs at the knees and walked, taking fast tiny steps. "Lower your center of gravity," he said, "and walk like you're squishing bugs. First rule: never stop moving. Second rule: never look down. *Never*. Throws off your balance. Keep your eyes on the horizon."

"Easy," I said. "I'll go first."

And I *was* first—to fall into the water.

But not this time.

I crouched and found my center of gravity, used my paddle to push off, and began gently rowing.

I kept my gaze on the island, but from the corner of my eye I could see that Greta had remembered Dawkins' lessons, too. We were all making good progress.

I cruised smoothly away from the pool's edge.

Sammy was the first to slip. I didn't see him go in—I had my eye on the horizon—but I heard his angry shout and a big splash, and then his orange float went shooting across the water right in front of me. It ricocheted off the island and floated away.

"One down!" Kieran shouted, followed by a shriek of maniacal laughter.

We'd all started pretty far apart, but the closer we got to the center, the closer we got to each other. When I reached the halfway point, I could see Blue, Greta, and Kieran without even having to turn my head.

Suddenly Blue shouted, "Hey! Knock that off!"

"Knock *you* off," Kieran said. A *smack*! And then a splash and Kieran laughed again. "Two down!" he crowed. "Best way to win is to eliminate the competition."

Dawkins would have praised Kieran's balance and skill with his paddle. His long strokes drove his float quickly across the water almost like it was a canoe.

Except he was steering himself straight at Greta.

"That's enough," I said, twisting hard and heading his way. We were about ten feet from each other, and Greta was only a foot or two out of reach of Kieran's oar.

"You'll never reach me in time, Truelove," Kieran said. "Not before I've knocked off your girlfriend."

"Not on the float I won't," I said, jamming my paddle down blade-first into the water.

Pole-vaulters usually have a long run-up before they stick their pole in the ground and jump. But I wasn't trying to go high, just far. There was a breathless second when my paddle was perfectly upright, motionless. I pivoted my weight around it and threw my legs as high as I could into the air before I let go.

It wasn't a very clean jump.

But it did the trick.

I arced over the water between me and Kieran. He tried to back up, but he'd barely moved at all before I slammed into him.

We went over in a tangle. Water flooded my nose and eyes in a cold, wet shock, and then my knees hit the bottom of the pool and I struggled to stand up.

Someone was holding me down.

An arm wrapped around my neck and squeezed, so I worked my feet under me and pushed off hard.

We broke the surface together, Kieran on my back. My paddle was floating within reach. I grabbed it, wrapped both hands around the shaft, and swung it over my head.

It connected with something soft.

"Ah!" Kieran shouted and let go, and I spun around. Water dribbled out of the barred slot in his face mask. His eyes above it were angry slits.

"You need to calm down," I said.

He didn't say anything in response, just growled and splashed after Greta.

"It's over!" I shouted.

But Greta wasn't defenseless, and she certainly wasn't stupid. Bobbing around her were all the abandoned floats. Taking a deep breath, she leapfrogged from float to float all the way to the grassy edge of the island.

With one final jump, she reached the pedestal and plucked up the wooden box. She raised it over her head and shouted, "I win!"

Nestor and Vaughn watched from the shore.

"All but one of you fell into the water," Vaughn said, clucking her tongue. "But three of you fell while battling each other, which is something we very much admire. You three will move forward. As for you, Samuel, you simply lost your balance."

"That's true," Sammy said.

"I'm afraid your time with us is at an end. Tonight you will pack your things and in the morning you'll be escorted off the estate."

Sammy nodded. "No problem."

"You have got to be kidding." Kieran reached up and wrenched off his mask, and I couldn't help but feel relieved to see his normal face again. "The Truelove kid was trying to be *heroic*, defending his girlfriend. Why does he get to move forward?"

"He is in," Vaughn snapped. "We are not going to explain ourselves to you or anyone else, Kieran."

At the house, Nestor informed us that since we had proved ourselves untrustworthy not once, but twice, we would not be allowed to roam freely in the house or on the grounds. "You will be locked in your rooms. Or you will leave the competition. Those are your two choices."

Greta, Sammy, and I looked at each other. We'd found the Damascene 'Scope. And Greta was winning this Glass Gauntlet. Wherever Dawkins had gone, he knew this was where he'd find us.

"Which will it be?" Nestor asked, shaking a keychain in our faces.

"I'm in till you throw me out," I said, crossing my arms.

"I'm not going anywhere," Greta said. "I've already won twice."

"And I've already washed out," Sammy said.

"It's barely four o'clock," Blue protested. "What about dinner?"

"Sandwiches will be brought up," Nestor said, leading us up the staircase. "It is lucky for you that your host,

Miss Glass, admires children who think and act for themselves."

But it was more than that, I knew now. Kieran had complained about my acting "heroic," like that was something unexpected in these tests.

What's so bad about being heroic? I wondered.

CHAPTER 12
DRASTICALLY DRASTIC MEASURES

Five minutes later, the connecting door from the next room swung open, and Sammy and Greta strolled in.

"Any news from KoalaKlub?" Sammy asked, as I flipped open the lid of the laptop.

I shook my head, hoping I didn't look as anxious as I felt. I had a day left to accept or reject my dad's offer. Surely one of the Guard would check KoalaLou's treehouse before then, right? "Same as before."

Greta set the two wooden boxes on the desk and opened them. The new box held another section of the Glass Gauntlet—what looked like the index and middle fingers, as well as most of the back of the hand. Like the thumb section, it was made of a strange transparent material like fogged-up glass and was veined with brass wires.

She pushed the finger piece against the thumb section, and, with a loud click, the two pieces snapped together. She slipped her fingers and thumb inside and flexed them. The segments moved against each other with a screechy ceramic sound, like a teacup scraping a saucer.

"I wonder what this Gauntlet thing does," I said.

"Whatever, I bet it's cool," Sammy said. "We need to make sure you win the other pieces."

"Who cares?" Greta said. "I like to win as much as anyone—"

"More than anyone," Sammy said.

"—but this competition is just too crazypants." She disassembled the Gauntlet and returned the pieces to their boxes. "Anywhere else, knocking someone into the pool or running on top of the maze would be called cheating. But here, they sort of encourage it."

"Not 'sort of,'" I said. "*Definitely.* But I checked through the Verity Glass—they're not Bend Sinister. They're just . . ."

"Bad people?" Sammy suggested.

"Yeah," Greta said, shivering. "*Terrible* people."

"I don't trust them," I said. "And I think staying here any longer without Jack is a bad idea."

"But that Patch Steiner guy and the rest of the Bend Sinister are out there," Sammy said, frowning. "It's safer in here. That's what Jack would say."

"Well, he's not here, and the situation has changed. For the worse."

"He really should have been in touch by now," Greta said. "I'm worried."

"Me too," I said. *What would Dawkins do?* I thought.

Greta was a Pure. As a Blood Guard, I was sworn to protect her. The tests were weird, sure, but they weren't deadly. Was she in more danger here or out there? But the whole reason we were here in the first place was to find a way to save *another* Pure—Flavia.

"We came here to find the Damascene 'Scope, right?" I said. "We've done that. Now it's up to the Blood Guard to get Flavia's soul, bring it here, and use the Damascene 'Scope to put it back into her body."

"And just *how* are they supposed to get her soul here?" Greta glared at me. "Ask your dad to please put it in the mail? Send him an invitation?"

I thought again about my dad's deadline. He thought he was calling all the shots. Maybe it didn't have to be that way. "You know, we *could* do that."

"What do you mean?" Greta said, her eyes narrowing.

I explained how I'd logged on to ILZ the night before and found the message from my dad.

"Oh-kay," Greta said at last. "I don't like that you're in contact with him—"

"I *hate* it," Sammy said. "I still have nightmares about him and that mask he wore. And Kieran's freak-show bite guard doesn't help."

"I am *not* in contact with him!" I logged on to ILZ, then moved aside so that they could see. "I read *one* email. I didn't write back."

"Wow," Sammy said after he read it. "Your dad really *is* the worst."

I leaned over and reread the email, too. My dad thought he was so clever in how he outsmarted my mom—maybe we could use that against him. "My mom found my dad by pretending to be me, right? Except Dad figured it out and got mad. But it's not too late to give him what he wants." Even saying that made me feel slightly sick.

"You," Greta said. "What he wants is *you*."

"Right. What would happen if I offered myself up."

"No way!" Sammy said.

"Seriously, Ronan," Greta said. "That's a horrible idea."

"No, it's not," I said. "*Listen*. If I write him back, he forgets about my mom and your dad, forgets about attacking the Blood Guard, and he hurries over here to get me, right? Except . . . we make sure the Blood Guard is waiting, by using KoalaKlub to let them know that the Bend Sinister are on their way." Even as I said it I wondered if it would really work.

"You're saying we set up exactly the same trap your mom tried to set up?" Greta asked, smiling a little.

"He expects traps from my mom, but not from *me*."

"Um, guys—you're overlooking something," Sammy said. "*We're* here."

"We'll be long gone," I said, grinning now. It finally felt like I was *doing* something that mattered. "We're going to bust out of this place tonight."

"We are?" Sammy asked. "How?"

"We'll swipe a car from that garage," I said, "and then Greta will drive us out of here. We'll leave a note for Jack to meet us somewhere far away from this place."

"You can *drive*?" Sammy asked Greta. "Why did I not know that?"

"You never asked!" she said.

I pulled the laptop over in front of me. "Let's send the note to my dad. The sooner we get him away from my mom and your dad and the rest of the Guard, the better I'll feel."

I opened a Reply field and typed.

OK I'll meet with you if you promise to leave mom and the rest of the Blood Guard alone. Deal? I'll trust you if you give me your word.

I had the cursor poised over the SEND button when Greta asked, "What if Dawkins comes back and is mad at us?"

"For what?" I asked. I clicked the trackpad. Immediately there was a *whoosh* sound as the email was sent. "It's not like we actually revealed anything."

"I guess not," Greta said. "And I suppose we have plenty of time to change our minds before—"

The computer chimed as a new email appeared in DorkLord2K1's inbox. It was one line: *Deal. I give you my word. Where are you?*

"That was scary fast," Sammy said.

I clicked REPLY and started to type a description of the Glass Industries estate, but then stopped. "How do we know he'll bring Flavia's soul with him?"

"We don't." Greta shrugged. "The Blood Guard gambled your dad would have it with him in Minneapolis, right? We're going to have to make the same bet."

"We don't have *time* to make a bet," I said, remembering what my mom had said about Flavia. "That's the whole reason they even tried this crazy plan to catch my dad—because Flavia is *dying.* We have to be sure he brings her soul with him."

"How are we supposed to do that?" Greta said. "If you ask for it, it will make him suspicious, and then he absolutely *won't* bring it."

"I can think of a way to convince him," Sammy said. "But you're not going to like it." He dragged the laptop back toward him. "How much you want to bet the Bend Sinister wants this Damascene 'Scope thing, too?" He quickly typed a couple of lines.

We're here to find a junky old gadget called the Damascene 'Scope that's supposed to be able to zap souls away or something. But whatever it's supposed to do, it doesn't work.

"What does that mean—'zap souls'?" Greta asked.

"Whatever he thinks it means," Sammy said, pointing at my dad's email. "He probably knows a lot more about it than we do. If he thinks it destroys souls, then maybe he'll want to use it to get rid of the soul he's already got."

"I don't like this," Greta said. "At all. I feel like we're betraying something. Like the sacred trust of the Blood Guard."

"No, we're not," I said. "This is exactly what the Blood Guard were trying to do. Their plan didn't work. Ours will." Maybe I was just tired of hiding from the Bend Sinister, but for the first time, I felt like someone who could

126

actually *be* one of the Blood Guard. "We can't run forever," I said. "We might as well choose how we face them."

"That's just an expression, right?" Sammy asked. "We're not *actually* going to face them?"

"Of course not!" Greta said.

"In that case . . ." Sammy reached across the keyboard and hit SEND, and the email whooshed away.

"So the countdown begins now." I swallowed. "We have to make sure the Blood Guard get here before my dad does."

"He's in Minneapolis," Sammy said. "That's how many hours away?"

"*Maybe*," Greta said. "He might not have arrived yet. For all we know, he's driving around in DC, or camped outside the walls of the Glass Estate."

All three of us looked at the darkness outside the windows of my room.

"No way," Sammy said with a nervous laugh. "We've got time to get out of here."

"But just in case . . ." I brought up KoalaKlub on the laptop. "We should get our message to the Blood Guard and Dawkins as soon as possible. Here's what I think we should write."

Hours later, after Sammy and Greta had gone back to their rooms, and I'd eaten my dinner of cold tomato soup and a sandwich, and the clock had struck one in the morning, I got out of bed.

I hadn't been sleeping; I was too worried. Or excited. I couldn't tell the difference anymore. Hopefully, we'd diverted my dad, helping save the Guard from the trap he'd planned. And maybe we'd even spring a trap of our own here at the Glass estate. But whatever happened, I wasn't going to be around to see it. My duty was to keep Greta safe, and that meant getting far away long before the Bend Sinister arrived.

I slid the laptop into my backpack and went through the connecting door into Sammy's room. He was waiting. He put Kieran's iPad into my pack, too, and promised, "I'll give it back later." Then the two of us went into Greta's. I opened the backpack to add the wooden prize boxes.

"I'm not taking those."

"But you won them," I said.

"The rules are that they go to the ultimate victor," Greta said. "That's not going to be me. I follow the rules."

"Okay," I said, and slung the pack over my shoulders.

Greta had already picked the lock to the hallway.

"There's a camera down at the other end," Sammy said, easing the door open a crack. The lights in the hallway outside were turned down low. "It does a super slow pan. When I give the signal, we hustle to the back staircase."

He counted down from three on his fingers and we moved silently down the hall, then descended the stairs to the first floor. We were at the back of the central corridor, the one between the museum on one side and the living quarters on the other.

I could barely see Greta and Sammy's faces in the dim light of the stairwell. Above their heads, someone had painted the word RAGE. Yet more unexplained weirdness in the Glass house.

"From here," I said quietly, "we sneak to the entry hall, through the sitting and dining rooms, into the kitchen, and out the back door we saw there."

"And then we just have to make it to the garage," Sammy whispered. "Across all that grass. Acres of grass."

He didn't need to say what we were all thinking: the dogs.

We hadn't even left the house yet, and already my heart was booming in my ears.

Sammy frowned. "Even if we run nonstop, it'll take us like fifteen minutes to get to that garage."

Would the dogs hear our footsteps and our ragged breathing? I could already see them in my head, four shadows appearing from the dark, all teeth and snarls.

"We'll never make it," I whispered.

"How else are we supposed to get there, Ronan?" Greta whispered back.

"Guys," Sammy said. "There's a better way." He pointed at the RAGE sign.

"We get angry?" I said.

Sammy snorted. "Dude, it says *garage*—or used to, probably. See the arrow?"

I could, now that he traced it with a finger: It pointed down. Farther along the back stairs, through a door, into a basement.

We found a tunnel there, stretching in front of us, caged bulbs mounted on the ceiling every couple hundred feet. Another tunnel went the other way, toward the front of the house.

"I wonder if that one goes to the estate entrance," Greta said. "Maybe we should just forget the garage and go the other way."

"Can't risk being wrong," I said. "Let's stick with the garage."

As we jogged down the tunnel, Sammy asked, "But how are we going to get past the front gates?"

"What would Dawkins do?" I asked.

I could hear the smile in Sammy's voice when he said, "Ram 'em."

Fifteen minutes later, the tunnel ended at a circular black metal staircase.

We climbed up and into a long building. In the faint light through the windows set in the garage doors, we could see eight or nine cars and vans in a row. Some were covered with tarps, others were up on jacks.

"Which one should we take?" I asked Greta.

"Depends. Which one has keys in the ignition?"

We went down the line, checking each of the cars without luck, until we got to the last, which was covered by a greasy canvas tarp. I tugged it off.

Next to me, Greta gagged. "Oh no."

It was the Forest Service truck. A long, jagged line of

bullet holes started at the flat front tire then zagged up the fender all the way to the shattered windows. I counted twenty shots before I quit counting, because by then I'd seen the blood splattered all over the seats.

"We have to go back," I said, feeling sick. "They've got Dawkins."

CHAPTER 13
YOU DON'T KNOW JACK

As we raced back through the tunnel, I stopped feeling sick. Instead, I felt *angry*. These Glass Industries people had tried to kill my friend. True, he couldn't be killed outright, but he still felt pain, and whatever they'd done to him, he had to be suffering. It was up to us to find him, rescue him, and make this Ms. Glass person pay. "We've got the rest of the night to find Jack and then get out of here before morning."

"Searching the house will take forever," Greta said.

"Kieran's iPad," Sammy said. "He mirrored Nestor's desktop on it. Once we're back in range of their wifi, I can piggyback on the surveillance system."

At the basement stairs, we looked down the other tunnel, the one that went toward the front of the estate. A cool breeze blew down the passageway.

"They might have him tied up down there somewhere," Greta said.

"First let's try Sammy's trick with the iPad."

At the top of the basement steps, I reached out to turn the doorknob only to have the door swing open in my face.

Light flooded the stairwell.

Blue rushed in, looking over her shoulder, and plowed right into me.

I clamped my hand over her mouth and swung her back inside the basement stairs. The door clonked shut behind us and we were in the dark again.

"Ronan!" Greta said, slapping my arm. "That's Blue!"

"*Shh*," I whispered, taking my hand away from her face. "We don't want them to hear us."

"You scared me," Blue said. She slid away along the wall until she was behind Greta.

"Sorry." I forced myself to smile. "What are you doing up?"

"Everyone's awake," she said. "They did a room check and found you guys were missing, then they locked us in again and now they're out looking for you."

"But they let you out?" Greta asked.

"You're not the only one who can pick a lock." Blue held up a twisted piece of wire.

"Swell," I said. "I wonder how long it'll be before they check the tunnels."

"Maybe a while," Blue said. "They're driving around outside on their little golf carts."

"So we've got some time. Let's search the house fast before they get back," I said, opening the door again.

All the lights were on in the empty main corridor.

"Search for what?" Blue asked.

"Our friend Jack," I said. "He—um, we found his car in the garage, with like twenty bullet holes in it."

"Twenty bullets?!" Blue said, covering her mouth. "How could he still be alive?"

"You don't know Jack," Greta said. "He's . . . really tough."

"If you say so," Blue said.

We ran down the corridor and turned left into the sitting room. The house was so brightly lit—every lamp turned on and all the chandeliers at full power—that it was easy to forget that it was barely three in the morning. I kept expecting to turn a corner and bump into Nestor or Vaughn. But Blue was telling the truth; no one was around.

"Maybe I should get some knives from the kitchen," Greta said. "I wonder if any of them are weighted for throwing."

"They're weighted for *cooking*," I said. "It's a kitchen, not an armory."

"We can set up in here," Sammy said, reaching into my backpack for Kieran's iPad. I took the laptop out, too, figuring that while he looked for Dawkins, I could check KoalaKlub.

"What are you guys doing?" Blue asked, watching as Sammy tapped the iPad's screen.

"Checking out the house and grounds," Sammy said. He studied each image before tapping the screen and moving forward to the next. "There's not much to see. Just lots of empty rooms and hallways."

I logged on and found a new message in chalk on the board.

WARNING REC'D
MEETING ABORTED
ON OUR WAY
XOMOM

I coughed.

"What is it?" Greta said, leaning over me so she could see the screen. "Oh, that's great! They're okay!"

"What's the good news?" Blue asked, peeking over my shoulder.

"A message from our parents," I said, slamming the lid closed. "It's a long story."

"But I thought you guys were orphans," Blue said, backing away. "Like me."

"Sorry," Greta said. "It's complicated, but we had to lie about that."

"To win a million dollars?" Blue said. "Yeah, I'm sure it's *real* complicated."

Sammy glanced at me. "No sign of Jack so far. I mean, these cameras don't have X-ray vision, so I can't look inside the rooms, but there's nothing suspicious in here or on the external cameras. Just Nestor and Vaughn on their golf carts, and that garage, and we know he's not there."

"We don't have *time* to search the entire house," I said,

"*Shh.*" Blue raised a finger to her lips. "*Listen.*"

A soft, rapid *tick-tick-tick* of claws on tile floor, a jingle of metal.

The Dobermans.

"Oh, come *on*," I whispered. "Sammy, did you spot the dogs on the external cameras?"

He grimaced. "No . . ."

"We need to hide."

"Dining room?" Greta said, already leading the way through the dining room, the rest of us right behind her. She pushed the swinging door closed. "It doesn't lock. Why doesn't it lock?"

Sammy went past her and said, "Kitchen!"

But that swinging door didn't lock, either.

From a room behind us came a blood-chilling growl.

"Outside?" Greta asked.

"No," I said, pointing. "In there. No one will hear us or look for us there."

"Because it's a *freezer*," Greta said, rubbing her hands up and down her arms. "Only an idiot hides in a freezer. Because people *freeze* to death in a freezer."

I found a light switch and flipped it, and two rows of fluorescents flickered on all the way to the back. The freezer was big, maybe thirty feet deep. Shiny steel racks were packed with sauces and parcels wrapped in white paper. At the back wall was a waist-high glassed-in case like the sort stores use to sell ice cream, and a huge stained wooden table. A row of bloody aprons hung from hooks.

Blue shivered and crouched down by the door. "I'm just going to wait here."

"Maybe if we huddle together, we can stay warm until it's safe to leave," Sammy said.

So we all sat in a close circle by the door and shivered quietly. Sammy took out the iPad, whispered, "I still have a signal," and showed us the kitchen. The camera must have been mounted up high: we could see everything, including the dogs sniffing around the freezer door.

Blue's teeth started chattering, and on the screen the dogs' ears perked up. Suddenly there was a scratching noise from the other side of the door.

"You've got to be kidding me," I whispered. "They can hear that?"

"Sorry," Blue said, and opened her mouth wide. Her breath came out in perfect little puffs of white.

"I don't know how long I can take this," Greta whispered. She was shaking, too.

"It's only been a couple of minutes," I said. "Let's give it fifteen."

The fluorescent light overhead buzzed and clicked. I closed my eyes and prayed my mom and the rest of the Blood Guard would arrive soon, so that we could leave this icy box.

Suddenly the silence was broken by the *bing-bong* of a cell phone.

I looked around.

On the wooden table was a plastic grocery store bag.

Bing-bong.

Greta and I ran to it, grabbed it by its bottom, and spilled out the contents: a wadded-up leather jacket, a pair of blood-soaked jeans, and a yellow YOLO T-shirt with the final letter X'd out in black marker. And in the pocket of the jeans, a sticky-with-blood phone. It was a familiar-looking bright orange with an exclamation-point center button.

On its screen was the latest of a half-dozen text messages:

Got coordinates. Coming.

And earlier:

Where are you?

Sammy and Blue quietly crouched down next to me and Greta.

"Is that blood?" Blue asked.

Greta just nodded. The only sounds as we scrolled backward through the messages were our breathing and the freezer's fans. I stopped feeling the chill of the room. All I could see was the phone's tiny screen.

The first three messages were all in a row from the night before

C U @ our place

Meet up?

Got # from koalaklub

"So Dawkins went to meet Ogabe," I said, "but he never made it."

"Who the heck is Ogabe?" Blue asked. She fluttered her hands. "And those bloody clothes—shouldn't we get help?"

"This stuff belongs to our friend," Greta said, blowing warm air into her clenched hands. "We need to find him."

I glanced at the fogged door of the cold case, then tried to wipe it clear, but the glass was misted over from the inside.

I exhaled and a cloud of my breath hung in the air in front of me.

From the inside.

"Jack!" I said, and yanked open the door.

Folded up in the bottom of the case, ropes around his wrists, ankles, and neck, lay Dawkins.

CHAPTER 14

I KNOW WHY THE CAGED GUARD SCREAMS

His face and body were covered with a white mask of frost, but I could still see little puckered circles of flesh—partly healed gunshot wounds, I figured. He was naked except for his boxer shorts and socks, and he was all skin and bones—thinner than I'd ever seen him. A band of silver duct tape covered his mouth.

"Jack!" I shouted.

His eyes flickered open and he raised one of his eyebrows.

I yanked the tape away, and he shouted "Ow!"—or tried to shout; it came out like a harsh whisper.

With Sammy and Greta's help, I lifted him out of the case and laid him down. He was shivering violently, his skull knocking against the floor. Greta stuffed his wadded-up clothes beneath his head. "We've got to do something to warm him up!"

His body was suddenly wracked by coughing, and he

turned and spat out a dark gray blob that *clonked* against the metal floor.

"He's sick," Blue said, backing up.

"He's *cold*," Greta said. She wrapped her arms around him. "We should warm him up with our body heat."

"Okay," Sammy said, hugging Dawkins from the other side.

"It's a bullet," I said, looking at the thing on the floor. "His body is working the slugs out of his system."

"Whoa." The frozen open-mouthed shock on Blue's face almost looked like a smile.

"Someone untie these ropes," Greta said, squeezing him tighter.

"Ouch," Dawkins moaned, his teeth chattering. "But warm."

"Blue, can you check the pockets of his jeans?" I asked. "He had a swiss army knife."

But Blue didn't move. She just kept staring.

"I'll get it." The Zippo lighter was in the front left pocket of Dawkins' pants, the swiss army knife in the right. I fumbled out the big blade and sawed through the ropes. Soon Greta had Dawkins sitting up, and the three of us all hugged him from different directions.

"Happy to see"—he coughed—"you, too. Ah, pardon me." Something rattled against his teeth and he gently spit out another slug.

"Oh, Jack," Greta said, "all this time you were down here—we didn't know."

"S'okay," he murmured. "Only a little frostbit."

He reached up, his hand shaking, and snapped ice out of his eyebrows, then pulled himself to his feet, leaning against the cold case for support. "You look," he said to Blue, "strangely familiar."

"Her name is Blue," Greta said. "You met her before. She's in the Glass Gauntlet with us."

"Don't think that was it," Dawkins said. He struggled to give her his winning smile. "Pleasure to meet you."

"You ought to put on some clothes," Blue said.

"Hey," Greta said. "Be nice! This is our friend you're talking to."

"No, she's right," Dawkins replied, giving Blue a long look. "I *am* practically in my altogether."

"Here," Sammy said, holding out an apron. "It's the cleanest one. Your clothes were shredded."

"Excellent," Dawkins said, slipping it over his neck and tying the strings behind his back. "Should we need to do any cooking, I'll be ready."

"It's not funny," Greta said.

"I don't suppose any of you brought along something to eat, by chance? I'm deliriously hungry."

"Sorry," I said. "We can eat once we get out of here. What happened?"

Dawkins fluttered his hand. "I went to meet Ogabe, but got only as far as the front gate. That thug Nestor stepped out and shot the truck to pieces."

"He shot you because you couldn't start the truck?" I asked.

"Of course not," Dawkins said. "He shot me because he *wanted* to shoot me. That's usually how these things work. Oh, and he took a certain something." Dawkins made a V with his fingers, and I knew right away what he meant: his Verity Glass. "The question is, who told him to do so? He's not the brightest bulb in the marquee, is your Mr. Nestor." I handed Dawkins the cell phone and he read through the messages. "Help is on the way. That's some good news, at least."

"There's more news," I said. "Worse news."

"Oh?" he said. "What could be worse than being stashed in a freezer like a cut of meat?"

"My dad and the Bend," I said. "They're *also* on their way."

Dawkins laughed in surprise. "I imagine there's a very good story behind—"

The door to the freezer was yanked open.

"Oh, *you* again," Dawkins said. "And your little toy."

Nestor was holding a machine gun. And it was aimed at us.

"How are you even alive?" Nestor gaped.

"I'm kind of stubborn that way," Dawkins said.

"So *this* is where you three have been hiding!" cooed Vaughn, appearing with the dogs. They strained at the leashes she held, until all of a sudden they quieted and sat down. "I'm afraid this violation of our rules disqualifies you from the Glass Gauntlet."

"That's okay," Greta said, watching as Dawkins coughed a bullet out onto the floor. "We quit."

◆   ◆   ◆

"Your elbow's in my gut!" Sammy said.

"Sorry!" Greta said. "Just trying to get comfortable."

"Mmmph," said Blue from somewhere below.

The five of us were crammed inside the telephone booth–sized cage in the Museum of Perceptual Inquiry. To our right was a vat with the dummy floating upside down in water, and on our left, a glass display case filled with crystal balls.

"Classic trick from the 1920s," Sammy explained. He rapped his knuckles on the metal bars. "These welded steel bars? Saws can't cut through them!"

"So how does the magician escape?" I asked.

"When the magician squeezes the right pressure points on the padlocks," Sammy explained, "they pop open."

"Unfortunately for you," Vaughn said, "we are not using those padlocks."

The cage was tall enough that Dawkins could stand up straight, and just wide enough that we could all barely fit snugged up against each other. Blue got stuck in the middle, crouching between our legs. She didn't seem to mind. "There's more room down here," she said. "People aren't so thick in the bottom parts."

A sudden horrifying growling made everyone freeze. Nestor raised the machine gun.

"Just my belly, sorry!" Dawkins said. "I don't suppose one of you could bring me a sandwich?"

"You suppose correctly," Vaughn said as Nestor marched off toward the hall's exit.

"Or perhaps I could speak with the mysterious Ms. Glass? Even that robot surrogate of hers would do."

"Please stop talking," Vaughn said. "Ms. Glass has spent a great deal of time and money making the Damascene 'Scope functional. Yet it requires something that money can't buy, something only you and your friends in the Blood Guard possess."

"Wit? Style?" Dawkins asked. "Good looks?"

I caught Greta's eye. So Ms. Glass knew about the Blood Guard. Did that mean she was part of the Bend Sinister? Is that why she wouldn't show herself—because she was afraid we'd be able to see her true colors with our Verity Glasses?

Vaughn whistled. There was a scrabbling of claws on tile and the four Dobermans loped in. They sat in a circle around us, panting and staring, their ears standing at attention.

"That must be why you took my Verity Glass," Dawkins mused. "But one Glass isn't enough, is it? The 'Scope requires three, if memory serves."

I slid my hand up to grasp mine through my shirt, but then realized someone might be watching and turned the gesture into a neck scratch.

"More than one of you was supposed to come for the 'Scope," Vaughn said. "Not one of you and a bunch of children." She looked at her watch. "It is four thirty in the morning, and there is much to be done. Thanks to the three of you being disqualified—"

"Don't forget me," Blue said.

"Correction: the four of you," said Vaughn with an odd smile. "We need to outfit our remaining student with the Gauntlet, train him in its use, and test him on the device. While we attend to that, we are going to leave you to the dogs. If you're foolish enough to try to escape, they *will* tear out your throats."

Her footsteps echoed along the hall, and then the door to the museum closed and we were alone.

One of the dogs yawned.

Okay, *almost* alone.

"What did she mean about training someone to use the Gauntlet?" Dawkins asked.

"It's an actual thing," Greta said. "This weird glove made out of glass, with brass wires running through it."

"Ah," Dawkins said, and closed his eyes. "*Lux chirotheca* in the literature about the 'Scope. It wasn't just dippy Victorian-era terminology. The hand of light is *literal*. It's real."

"That glass glove is part of the Damascene 'Scope?" I asked.

"Apparently," Dawkins said. "Though it's anyone's guess how it functions in concert with the device."

"What is he babbling about?" Blue asked.

"Never you mind," Dawkins said, opening his eyes and shaking his head. "I forgot we had a stranger among us. Greta, why don't I lift you up so you can reach those locks and pick them and get us all out of here?"

"I can't," Greta said, frowning. "Those are Abloys—they're almost unpickable. Without the right tools, I'll never get 'em open."

"And anyway," I said, sticking my arm through the cage and pointing, "there's these guys."

All four dogs growled and bared their fangs, their eyes fixed on my hand.

I slowly pulled my arm back. "Easy, boys."

"I love dogs, Ronan," Dawkins said. "And they absolutely adore *me*." He whistled a series of soft high-pitched notes that hurt my ears. A moment later, the dogs came up to the cage, wagging their tails and whining. Dawkins reached through and they licked his hand. "Who's a good boy?" he said over and over. "That's right! It's *you*."

"Wow," Blue said. "How in the heck did you do that?"

"Dogs and Jack just get along," Greta said. "But that still doesn't solve the problem of how we get out of this thing."

"What if we rock back and forth and tip over the cage?" Sammy suggested.

"That would just make us all very uncomfortable," Dawkins said.

And then I remembered something: Nestor and Vaughn hadn't bothered to search us. "Hey, I've still got your swiss army knife. Can you use that to pick the locks, Greta?"

"Sorry, Ronan," Greta said. "I'd need a lock pick set. And, like, a couple hours."

"I've still got Kieran's iPad," Sammy said, pulling up his shirt and sliding it out. "And . . . it's still patched in to the surveillance system. See? There's Nestor sitting at his security desk."

I twisted around until I could see the camera feed from the central corridor. A blobby version of Nestor had his legs up and his head down. "He's sleeping!" I said.

"It *is* the middle of the night," Greta said. "It's what people usually do."

"This gives rise to a very unpleasant idea about how we might get the keys," Dawkins said, still scratching the dogs' heads. He sighed. "Ronan, give me that knife."

"Here's how this is going to work," Dawkins said a second later, folding out the longest blade.

With his left hand, Dawkins gripped the bar of the cage before him. "First I am going to whisper an incantation that, had your training been further along, you three would have learned." I remembered my mom muttering a spell in the front seat of our VW, just before she burst out of the car and straight into a hail of bullets. "It adds to the tensile strength of a weapon—enables it to deflect bullets, for example. But the spell also gives the blade a supernatural edge, allowing it to cut through most things as though they were Kleenex."

"So you're going to cut the bars?" Blue asked.

"Alas, no," he rapped the blade against the bar. "Sammy is right about these tempered steel bars. Even enchanted, the blade of this pocketknife can't cut through that."

Sounding sick, Greta said, "Blue—turn toward the back wall. Jack, are you sure you have to do this?"

He nodded. "The cutting should go fast. Once I start, I suggest all of you scream and shout. Really raise a ruckus. That should provide cover for *my* screams."

All of a sudden I understood. I'd seen Ogabe's head reattached to his body, so I knew any wound Dawkins suffered would not be permanent. But that didn't make the idea any less sickening. "No, Jack," I whispered. "You don't have to cut off your hand!"

"His *hand*? Why would he do that?" Blue asked, and then to Dawkins, "Won't you die?"

"Fortunately—or unfortunately—no," Dawkins said. He began a hoarse whispering. Within moments, the three-inch blade of the swiss army knife flickered with a pale blue glow.

Sammy and I pushed away to give him room, while Greta reached down and covered Blue's eyes.

"Knock that off!" Blue said. "I want to *see*."

"No, Blue," Greta said. "Ronan, help me."

While Blue wiggled against our legs, the two of us blocked her line of sight.

"Now would be a good time to make some noise," Dawkins said. He pressed the blade down against the narrowest part of his wrist. "Here goes."

I sucked in a big lungful of air, and we all screamed as long and as loud as we could.

CHAPTER 15

A HAND WHEN WE NEED IT MOST

The wet thud of something plopping to the ground made us stop.

Sammy groaned. "I don't want to look."

Our screaming had woken Nestor—I'd watched on the screen as his head snapped up and his feet dropped to the ground. He was just standing when we went quiet, and he stood looking off-camera for a minute, thinking.

The knife clattered to the floor of the cage, and Dawkins slumped against me. His face was pale and slick with sweat.

"He passed out," Greta said, swallowing. "But he did the job."

"But why?" Blue asked.

On the iPad, Nestor walked out of the frame. "Come on, Jack. Wake up." But then Nestor reappeared and sat back down at his desk.

"Please, Jack," Greta said, and then she reached around and slapped his face.

"Kittens!" Dawkins shouted as he came to. He looked down, sighed, and said, "Oh, yes. I remember now."

"Stay, boys!" Dawkins commanded the dogs.

"One of them is a girl," Greta pointed out. "Debra."

"No one likes a know-it-all, Greta," Dawkins said.

I watched as Dawkins' hand crawled, spiderlike, between the four dogs.

One dog whined softly, but Dawkins whispered "*Shh*," and it quieted.

The fingers almost seemed to ripple as the hand scuttled along the tile. It reached the closed door to the entry hall, pried at the edge, and then flattened and tried to crawl under.

"No go." Dawkins let out a pent-up breath. "Now what? I can't very well climb up and turn the doorknob."

I glanced at Nestor on the iPad. He was awake, but as I watched, he leaned back in the chair to resume his nap. "Knock," I said. "Just knock."

Grimacing, Dawkins tilted his head.

On the other side of the room, his hand rolled back onto the stump of its wrist, curled into a fist, and rapped three times on the door's bottom edge.

On the monitor, Nestor's head shot up, startled. He stood and looked at the closed doors of the museum.

"Come on, you lazy dodo," Dawkins said.

The hand rapped again, harder than before.

Nestor reached onto his desk and picked up the machine gun, then seemed to second-guess himself and picked up a blunt-nosed instrument instead: a Taser. He slowly approached the door.

"Here he comes," I said.

Across the room, Dawkins' hand scuttled along the baseboard and into the shadows under a display case.

"Everyone look natural!" Dawkins said, crossing his arms and tucking the stump of his wrist under his elbow. Where he'd made the cut, the skin had already sealed itself. "Or as natural as one can be while standing in a cage with a half-naked man in a butcher's apron who's just chopped off his own hand."

Nestor pushed open the door, his weapon at the ready. The four dogs looked back.

"Why, hello!" Dawkins called. He was sweaty and unsteady on his feet, but that probably wasn't visible from across the hall. "What you got there? Is it a sandwich? Ah, no, it's just a Taser. Talk about disappointments!"

"Somebody knocked on the door," Nestor said.

"A bit of a reach for us," Dawkins said.

"We're kind of in a cage over here," Greta said. "In case you haven't noticed."

Nestor edged over the threshold, sweeping the Taser back and forth, until he seemed satisfied that we were still locked tight in the cage. "I could have sworn someone knocked."

At his feet, the hand rose onto its fingertips, scampered along the wall, and disappeared out the door. I watched on the iPad as it scuttled the twenty feet to the security station.

"I hear phantom noises all the time," Dawkins said, glancing at the iPad. "Police sirens. Dinner gongs. Gabriel's trumpet." The hand used the drawer pulls to hoist itself up to the surface of the security desk.

"Whatever you say, funny guy," Nestor said, lowering the Taser. "Just know that I'm right outside. And I'll be listening." He pushed the door wide, then disappeared back down the hall.

Dawkins leaned in close to watch on the iPad.

On the desk, the hand crawled back and forth in a panic until finally Dawkins said "Aha!" His hand dove deep into a dish of mints and dug down, burying itself.

"What if he wants a mint?" Sammy asked.

"I can't taste them, but these things *feel* like chalk," Dawkins said. "Trust me, no one would ever eat one voluntarily."

Between us, Blue said, "Can all of you guys do that—cut yourself into pieces?"

"Ugh, no!" Greta said. "Jack's just . . . talented." To Dawkins, she said, "Now what?"

"Patience, Greta Sustermann." Dawkins made a series of low sounds deep in his throat.

Immediately the dogs erupted into a wild, terrifying howling, throwing themselves at the cage and snapping their teeth. I'd thought there was no extra room in the cage, but suddenly we all squeezed tighter in the center, away from the edges.

"Excuse me!" Dawkins shouted. "Machine Gun Eddie—yoo-hoo!"

Nestor rose from his chair and again walked out of frame.

He appeared in the doorway and waved the machine gun at us. "Do you want more of this?"

"These dogs!" Dawkins yelled. "They won't stop nipping at our hands."

Nestor called to the dogs and they immediately stopped barking. "So keep your hands to yourself and you won't have a problem. But bother me again, and I *will* shoot you. Got it?"

We watched on the iPad as Nestor strolled back to his desk, only to stop in shock when he saw what was waiting for him: Dawkins' hand covered in mint dust, propped against the phone and aiming the Taser straight at Nestor's chest.

"Hello, sweetheart," Dawkins said.

And then the hand squeezed the trigger.

After Dawkins' hand brought us Nestor's keys, and after Sammy climbed onto my shoulders so that he could reach the locks, and after we got out of the cage at last, Dawkins plucked a purple silk scarf from a display and gave it to me. Then he picked up his hand and held it against his wrist. "Tie this up, Ronan, would you?"

I knotted the scarf as tight as I could around his wrist.

"This will take some time to knit itself back together, but it should hold for the nonce." He crouched down and nuzzled the dogs. "Such good boys!" he said. "Even you, and you're a girl!" He turned to us. "Let's get out of here before your dad shows up."

"There's a tunnel to the garage," I said. "We can get a car there."

"Excellent," Dawkins said, "though maybe I should grab some proper clothes first." He pointed to Nestor lying unconscious on the floor. "A bit stuffy for my tastes, but in a pinch, you take what's on offer."

We stripped off his coat and pants, and then Sammy and I dragged Nestor into the museum and locked him in the cage. Dawkins bent and whispered into the dogs' ears, and, wagging their tails, they again sat in a circle. "They'll make sure Nestor doesn't try to get out when he wakes up."

"Oh, and we found the Damascene 'Scope," I said, grabbing my backpack from under the desk.

Dawkins stopped and looked at me, his mouth open. It took me a half second to realize that he was too surprised to speak. "Why didn't you say so?" he said at last. "Where is it?"

"It's in a crate on a cart over there," I said, pointing.

"Then I'll just go retrieve my Verity Glass and we'll get gone," Dawkins said, heading back into the museum.

I followed him. He threw the tarp aside and pushed the lid of the crate to the ground, then ran his fingers lightly over the shiny brass of the 'Scope. He whistled softly. "That Vaughn person wasn't kidding: a lot of work has been done modernizing this thing." Dawkins rotated the 'Scope in its crate, revealing a glass-windowed port that opened like the back door of a hatchback. Within, rows of glass disks— lenses—were mounted on brass tracks. "Optics in the Victorian era was a young science, and even the best lenses they could make were still no better than the smudgiest of windows."

I pivoted out one of the lens plates. "Here's your Verity Glass."

"Thank you, Ronan." He popped it out of the brass filigree and slid it into his sock, then blew out a puff of air. "We really should take this with us."

"How would we carry it? Doesn't it weigh like four hundred pounds?"

"You're right, of course: it's impractical to take the 'Scope with us now. We'll just have to come back for it. I'm afraid my recent traumas, as well as the lack of a square meal, has left me a bit foggy. Feel free to boot me in the rear whenever necessary."

"You got it," I said.

"Don't look so delighted," he said, "I didn't mean that *literally*."

From the doorway, Greta, Blue, and Sammy watched impatiently. "Guys," Sammy said, "We've got company."

As we walked up, he tapped the screen and zoomed in on an image from the front entrance.

"Oh, for the love of Pete," Dawkins said. "Why'd your father have to send *him*?"

On the other side of the gate, an SUV had stopped. Out climbed several people in suits. Two helped a sixth person out of the backseat—a familiar-looking fat man in a bowler.

Patch Steiner.

CHAPTER 16

A VERY OLD FRIEND

"Nestor's not there to let them in," Sammy said. "They're stuck on that side of the gate."

"How fortunate for us!" Dawkins said.

But as we watched, Steiner and his team of agents formed a line, spoke some sort of incantation, and raised their glowing hands into the air. The metal of the gate brightened until it was white-hot, then it seemed to liquefy and ripple away from a central hole, like the water in a pond after a stone is thrown in.

"I knew that was too convenient," Dawkins said, wobbling slightly. "Time we picked up the pace, gang. I'd rather we not be within range of that blind giant's weird powers."

I flashed on how, only two days ago, Steiner had stolen my balance, my sight, and my ability to walk. Was he like a dog with a scent? Could he sense me already? "Let's hurry—the garage."

"What powers?" Blue asked.

"We'll explain later," Greta said. "Right now, we've got to run."

"We can take the tunnel," Sammy said, leading the way to the back of the corridor.

But on reaching the landing at the bottom of the basement stairs, Dawkins held us back, whispering, "Quiet, everyone." He cupped a hand to his ear.

We stood still and listened. From somewhere up ahead, too far away to be seen: heavy footsteps.

"Where's this other tunnel go?" Dawkins whispered, pointing behind us.

"We don't know," I said, shrugging. "To the front of the estate, maybe?"

"It goes to the hedge maze," Blue said.

"That's in the right direction," Dawkins said, shrugging. "Everyone proceed quickly and quietly, and let's hope that whoever is coming from the garage heads up into the house instead of after us."

After fifteen minutes of walking quietly, Dawkins shushing us whenever anyone tried to talk, Greta whispered, "Maybe Ms. Glass is working with . . . them. And that's why Patch Steiner showed up."

Dawkins shook his head. "This just doesn't *feel* like one of their operations. The sense I got was that Steiner had one task: to capture Ronan for his dad."

I must have made a sound, because Dawkins added,

"It's okay, Ronan. We'll just hide out in that maze until morning. If none of our friends have shown up by then, we will find some other way off the grounds."

"You have friends coming?" Blue asked. "Do they have purple monocles, too?"

Over Blue's head, Dawkins gave me a weird sideways look. "What a strange question. Why do you want to know?"

"Just wondering," Blue said. "Ronan has the one his mom gave him, and now you have the one you took out of that telescope—did his mom give that one to you, too?"

"Um," I said, trying to figure out an explanation for why Dawkins also had what I'd told Blue was a family heirloom.

"We're here," Greta said, saving me.

The cement-walled tunnel opened into a sort of silo with a metal staircase like the one under the garage. Overhead was a domed metal roof.

"How are we supposed to get out?" I asked.

Blue pointed to a gray metal box on the wall. A red bulb was lit next to a dark green one; between them was a key turned to CLOSE. "Maybe just crank it to 'Open'?"

"So sensible!" Dawkins said, twisting the key.

The stairwell filled with noise—gears grinding over our heads and some kind of engine whining—and the hatch above us began to open up, a tiny hole at the center growing like a pupil dilating in an eye, forming a round hatchway about eight feet across. A breeze blew down through the opening.

"Ronan and I will go first, Greta, if you don't mind," Dawkins said, shouldering past her.

I followed him out onto the grassy hill at the center of the maze, right behind the stumpy little tree, the stone pedestal, and the old water hose. There was the faintest smudge of light in the sky. Dawn wasn't far off.

Dawkins suddenly flopped down onto the grass. I felt like doing the same thing.

From somewhere far away, we could hear the ringing of an alarm.

"That doesn't sound good," I said, sitting down next to Dawkins and staring at the dark, dead hedges. The maze was still arranged as Vaughn had left it, with one straight pathway from the outside edge to the center.

"You think that alarm is because of us?" Greta asked, her head coming up through the hatch.

She and Blue and Sammy climbed out and stood looking back toward the house.

"Oh, it's most definitely because of you," Patch Steiner said, walking out from behind the nearest hedgerow.

I looked back at Dawkins and realized that he'd fallen over not because he was tired, but because of something Steiner had done to him.

"Leave Jack alone," I said, standing up.

Steiner gestured for me to sit. "Now, now, Evelyn, I'd rather no one get hurt. Which is why I've immobilized Mr. Dawkins until we have you and your friends in custody."

"Who *is* this guy?" Blue whispered, sliding behind me. "What's he done to your friend Jack?"

"He can steal people's senses," Sammy said. "Even their sense of balance."

"*Equilibrium* is a better word," Steiner said. "And in this case, I stole Mr. Dawkins' *proprioception*, his sense of self—basically, I've trapped him inside his own body. It no longer understands how to communicate with his brain." Behind Steiner came three of his agents, one jabbing the muzzle of a Tesla rifle into Vaughn's back. She had her hands raised over her head.

"How did you find us?" I asked.

"Why, Evelyn—it was *you* who told your father you were here."

I was almost grateful that Dawkins couldn't move so that I wouldn't have to see his face. I still hadn't had time to explain: this was all my fault. I'd been so stupid, so sure I could outsmart my dad that I'd outsmarted myself. I'd trusted him to come alone instead of sending one of his Hands. I'd endangered all of my friends, and now we were at Steiner's mercy.

"Oh, but you mean *here*, in this hedge maze, don't you?" the big man went on. "Why, the surveillance system, of course! We saw the five of you stroll past one of the tunnel cameras, so we simply drove over."

"Okay," I said. "I'll go with you. Just leave my friends alone."

"Alas, I am no longer so trusting," Steiner said, wheezing

slightly as he climbed the slope. "You made things very difficult for me in Wilson Peak, and I will not disappoint Head Truelove again." He walked right up to me and clucked his tongue. "Mr. Five here is going to handcuff each of you, and once I'm convinced you pose no threat, I'll release Mr. Dawkins."

One of the dark-haired men with him silently held out a pair of handcuffs. Greta raised her wrists, and the man snapped them shut. He bent down, pulled Dawkins' arms around, and then cuffed his hands as well.

Sammy was next, and then me. As the man closed the first cuff around my wrist, Blue said, "So this fat man is doing something to Jack to keep him down?"

"Indeed I am, little girl," Steiner said with a chuckle. "You'll find I am quite formidable."

"We'll see about that," Blue said. From behind her back she drew out the Taser from the security desk. I hadn't even seen her pick it up.

Two little darts shot out trailing electrical wires. The darts struck Steiner's massive belly and the gun buzzed and crackled.

Steiner trembled, said "Oh my," and fell over.

"That. Was. Sweet," Sammy said.

Immediately, Steiner's team of agents went blank. Their arms dropped, their grips relaxed, and their heads fell forward. Without their Hand, I remembered, they had no brain, like puppets with their strings cut. This was our chance.

At the foot of the hill, Vaughn picked up the Tesla rifle and cracked the stock of it against one of her captor's heads. He quietly fell over. Before he'd hit the ground, she turned on the female Bend Sinister agent, knocking her over, then using her handcuffs to lock the two agents together.

Blue hit a button on top of the Taser and the wires fell away. Then she jammed the contacts into Mr. Three's belly and pulled the trigger. The gun crackled and buzzed, and Mr. Three flinched and collapsed.

Dawkins sat up and rubbed his face with his cuffed hands. "You really are the most impressively nasty nine-year-old I've ever met." Greta helped him to his feet. "I'm very grateful, but I feel that you haven't been entirely honest with us."

"You have a good point there," Blue said. "For one thing, I am *not* actually nine." She smiled at Vaughn climbing the hill toward us. "Did you free Nestor before coming after us?"

"Yes, Ms. Glass." Vaughn carefully aimed the Tesla gun at Dawkins. "But two more of the fat man's team forced him and the dogs to take them through the tunnels. Just in case they missed you up here."

"Blue?" Greta asked. "What's going on?"

"My name isn't Blue, dear," Blue said, her voice sliding into a strange lilt.

"Why are you talking funny?" I asked.

"Because she's dropped her fake accent," Dawkins said.

"Where is it I know you from?"

"I honestly thought I'd never see you again, Jack." Blue kneeled and reached into his sock, withdrawing his Verity Glass. "I'll be needing yours, too, Ronan."

I froze, confused. "But you . . . ?"

She smiled and held out her open hand. "Don't make me hurt you, Ronan."

I tugged the chain over my head and gave the glass to her. She took it and then, almost as an afterthought, snapped the second handcuff around my wrist. To Vaughn, she said, "At least one more of the Blood Guard is on the way. He will have the third Verity Glass we need." Then she turned and started down the grassy slope.

"Come along, children," Vaughn said, pointing the way with the muzzle of her gun. "The cart is parked right outside the maze."

"How is it that I know her?" Dawkins muttered.

In front of us, Patch Steiner groaned, drawing everyone's attention.

Or almost everyone.

At that moment Dawkins threw himself backward into the darkness of the open hatchway. The metal steps rang out as his body bounced down, and we could hear him shouting "Ow! Aah! Och!" and then Vaughn shoved us aside and pulled the trigger on the Tesla gun.

But Dawkins was already gone.

The bolt crackled out across the mouth of the hatchway, blinding all of us.

Clasping my hands together I swung them around and into Vaughn as hard as I could. She grunted and dropped the rifle. Sammy grabbed it and spun, flinging it behind us.

"Follow Jack!" I said.

We scrambled through the hatch to the basement level. Dawkins was lying in a heap at the foot of the stairs. I leaped over him, lunged at the control box, and twisted the key back to CLOSE. The green light blinked out, the red light blinked on, and the noises of the hatch closing started up.

Blue's voice chased after us.

"It's flattering that you *almost* recognize me, Jack," she called. "After a hundred and eighty years I'd expect you to remember nothing of that day you abandoned me and Spinks."

"Agatha," Dawkins croaked, peering up at the little girl who stood looking down at us through the door's rapidly shrinking opening. "It's you, isn't it?"

She smiled. "Why, Jack, you *do* remember." Her smile disappeared a moment before the closing door obscured her face.

But we could still hear her when she said, "Too late."

CHAPTER 17

WE MAKE SOME UNWISE MOVES

In the pitch-dark of the stairwell, we suddenly heard a short scratching noise, and with a *pfft* a flame appeared: Dawkins' Zippo lighter. He held it high in his chained hands, and we huddled around him on the cold cement floor.

"Are you okay?" Greta asked.

He didn't look so hot. His limbs were bent in ways that arms and legs aren't supposed to go, and his hair was matted with wet blood.

"A bit busted up here and there, but nothing that time and a bathtub-sized bowl of soup won't mend," he said, wincing and propping himself against the cinder block wall. "Sadly, we have neither of those things."

The hatch above us was now fully closed, locking Agatha, Vaughn, and Steiner outside, but locking us inside, too. Aside from the Zippo's flame and the glowing red light on the hatch control, the stairwell was completely dark. The lights that had been on in the tunnel when we'd come this way before were now out.

"You know Blue—or . . . Agatha?" I asked. And at the same moment, I remembered a story he'd told us at the start of the summer. "That can't be . . . that's not the same—?"

"Girl from my childhood? Yes, it is." He grimaced and said, "Just a moment." Sweat broke out on his face as his crooked left leg jerked and shivered. There was a series of loud, grinding *cracks*, and then his leg was straight again. "Aaaah!" he breathed between clenched teeth. "Compound fractures are the absolute worst."

"But she looks like a nine-year-old," Greta said, taking a seat on the bottom step. "And yet you supposedly knew her like two hundred years ago?"

"And *I* look like a remarkably handsome nineteen-year-old," he said. "I'd wager her appearance has something to do with the Blood Guard and the Damascene 'Scope, and with this little competition she's put together, though the *why* of that remains out of—" He scowled. "Ah, here go the ribs." With a series of *pops* like someone snapping bubble wrap, his chest jerked one way and another until he was sitting up straighter. He let out a loud, ragged breath. "That's *some*what better."

I looked over at the dim mouth of the tunnel that led to the house. "Vaughn told Blue—"

"Agatha," Dawkins said.

"Agatha, right. She said that two of Steiner's agents made Nestor and the dogs lead them here through the tunnel."

"Give me a hand, would you?" Dawkins said. I reached out, and he pulled himself upright. "When Agatha Tased Steiner, it staggered all of his lackeys. Even the ones down here. Nestor's not smart, but even *he* would know to turn tail and run."

"I think Steiner was waking up," Sammy said. "He groaned."

"Which means he's now probably running Agatha 'round like a mouse in a maze. She had no idea what she was tangling with up there."

"But we don't have any weapons," I said.

"We'll improvise. First let's get free of these cuffs, and then—"

A clink of metal hitting the ground and Greta said, "I was practically out of them up there anyway, before everything went crazy."

"Nicely done, Houdini," Dawkins said, handing me the lighter. "Oh, fiddlesticks—behind you." He shoved Greta to the left just as a long, thin sword point jabbed into the chamber and straight through Dawkins' right side.

"That smarts," Dawkins said, then yanked the man's head forward against his knee. He released him and the man fell backward, unconscious.

Right into the path of the second agent, a redheaded woman with a saber.

She smiled. "You've been wounded, Mr. Dawkins."

"A minor inconvenience," Dawkins said, wincing and drawing the blade from his abdomen, "but worthwhile, because now I have a sword!" He swung it around just in time to parry her attack.

"You weaken with each thrust of your weapon!" she said, slashing at him. It was Steiner, I realized, speaking through his agent. "It is only a matter of time before I destroy—"

"Oh, put a sock in it," Dawkins said, driving her back. "Everyone, behind me."

The agent's chops and slashes with the blade steadily pushed Dawkins into a corner. And then with a snap of her wrist, the woman's sword sent Dawkins' spinning away.

She laughed. "You have run out of luck, Mr. Dawkins."

Dawkins hooked his pinkies around his lower lip, and blew hard, but no sound came.

"Are you trying to whistle?" She swished her blade. "Because I didn't hear anything."

Dawkins held his hands palm out. "Give it a moment."

Four sleek black shadows burst from the mouth of the tunnel.

Each of the Dobermans latched on to one of the agent's limbs, and, snarling, the dogs dragged her into the space under the staircase. She twisted and fought, but they locked their jaws and held tight.

"Jack—catch!" cried a familiar voice.

A sword came spinning end over end out of the tunnel. Dawkins raised his hands together, easily plucked the hilt from the air, then brought the blade point-down toward the woman's throat. "Easy, boys!" he said. And then a moment later, "And girl."

The four dogs calmed but didn't release the agent's arms and legs.

"You won't be able to escape, Mr. Daw—" The agent convulsed and then went limp.

Dawkins laughed. "Looks like Agatha got the jump on Steiner again. Ronan, Sammy, grab Greta's handcuffs and lock this redheaded charmer to the staircase, would you? And Greta?" He held out his own cuffs again.

As we did that, Ogabe appeared from the shadowy mouth of the tunnel, dragging Nestor by the scruff of his neck. The man was still only half dressed in his socks, underwear, and fancy dress shirt.

"Sit," Ogabe said. Without a word, Nestor did as he was told, even going so far as to cuff himself to the stairs. Ogabe dusted off the sleeves of his pin-striped suit. "How are you doing, friend?"

"To be perfectly honest," Dawkins said, "I've seen better days."

"You're wearing my clothes!" Nestor said.

"You noticed!" Dawkins said, looking down at himself. "Sorry about all the blood."

"I came in over the back wall, then made my way through the tunnel that connects the house to the garage," Ogabe explained.

"Ah, that was you we heard," Dawkins said.

We were walking down the long, cold tunnel that led to the house—Dawkins and Ogabe in the lead, each bearing a saber, the dogs frolicking around them, then Greta and Sammy, and finally me taking up the rear with the short sword the first agent had used to stab Dawkins.

"A shame we missed each other," Ogabe said. "But I saw those three and followed them. Halfway there, the two Bend Sinister agents went into convulsions—"

"Our host Tased their Hand," Dawkins said.

"That explains it," Ogabe said. "After they collapsed, the half-naked guy ran away down the tunnel and straight into me. Jack, I have to ask: What in tarnation is going on here?"

"Our safe, simple little mission was neither of those things," Dawkins told Ogabe. "While you were faffing about searching for the Grand Architect, we four were coping with not just one, but two different monsters. A massive fat one, and a wee tiny one—but both deadly."

"All Bend Sinister?" Ogabe asked.

"Those two back there are, of course. They belong to a Hand with a terrifying talent; he is able to steal another's senses. He's not alone, either; he still has three agents doing his biding.

"Our other opponent is . . ." We walked quietly for a few more steps. "She's someone I knew back when I was a boy. She looks about nine but is, like me, closer to two hundred. She's not an Overseer, but something must have

172

happened to her to stop her from getting any older." He shook his head. "We'll find out. Anyway, the half-dressed bald guy back there is one of hers, as is a trigger-happy harpy named Vaughn."

"They're armed?" Ogabe asked.

"To the teeth. Tesla rifles, machine guns, knives and swords, petty insults—a full arsenal." He clapped Ogabe on the shoulder. "But we can handle all of that! We have two Blood Guard Overseers, along with three plucky trainees, four adorably bloodthirsty Dobermans, and whatever army of Blood Guard you brought with you."

"I came alone."

"Splendid!" Dawkins swished his blade through the air. "My kind of odds."

The junction where the two tunnels met up in the basement was well lit and empty.

"The wise move would be to continue on to that garage," Dawkins said, pointing, "and either hide there until the rest of the Blood Guard arrive, or better yet, hijack a vehicle in which to make good our escape."

"We can't leave yet," Greta said. "We have to save Kieran."

"Like heck we do," Sammy said. "That kid is cray-zee. He wears this freaky painted mask that's all teeth and gore and I guess it's a good thing because it stops him from *biting* people."

"He's a total psycho," I said.

"None of that matters," Greta insisted. "He's not evil; he's just a little out of control. If anything happens to him, we'll be as much to blame as Agatha. She has something awful planned for him, I just know it."

"Someone please bring me up to speed," Dawkins said, rubbing his temple with his free hand. "Something about a psychopath in a mask who Greta wants to rescue?" From the look on his face, I knew what Dawkins was thinking: How could he convince Greta to let herself be protected without letting on to her *why* she had to be protected?

The three of us took turns talking, until Dawkins finally raised his hands to silence us. "So these tests reward *cheating?*"

"Not exactly," Greta said, thinking. "More like . . . ruthless kids. Ones who will hurt their opponents, or do whatever it takes to get what they want."

"But Greta," Dawkins said, "*you* won."

"But she wasn't *supposed* to win," I said. "Kieran would have beat her up in the maze if I hadn't tackled him. And he was going after her in the pool, too."

"I won because my friends had my back," Greta said.

"This Kieran boy sounds like a real keeper," Dawkins said. He looked down the tunnel to the garage, and then tipped his head back to look at the ceiling. "What does Agatha need with a ruthless, friendless, penniless, orphaned child? What does such a person offer her? Does he have anything to do with the Damascene 'Scope?"

"Jack." Ogabe spread his arms wide. "You said it your-self: the wise move would be to continue on to the garage."

Dawkins' old grin burst across his face. "And when have you ever known me to be *wise*?"

CHAPTER 18

A REFLECTIVE MOMENT

Using the iPad, Sammy cycled through views from the house's cameras.

There was no one in the sitting room, dining room, or kitchen; nor was there anyone at Nestor's desk in the corridor under the staircase or in the Museum of Perceptual Inquiry. The upstairs hall was empty, all of the doors open wide except Kieran's. "Looks like Kieran is still in his room," Sammy said. "Probably still asleep."

"The place looks abandoned," I said.

"Abandoned is good," Dawkins said. "Maybe Steiner and Agatha are keeping each other busy out in the maze. Gives us time to go grab this lunatic of yours and get out."

We climbed the stairs quietly—Dawkins and Ogabe in the lead; the dogs, Greta, and Sammy in the middle; and me covering the rear—then gathered around Kieran's door in the second-floor hallway. Dawkins made a low noise in his throat, and the dogs sat at attention.

"You want me to pick the lock?" Greta whispered. "Because I can do that, no problem."

"No, thanks—I prefer a more traditional approach," Dawkins said. He held his sword behind his back, then with his other hand, rapped out three sharp knocks. "Good morning, Kieran!"

"Who's there?" Kieran said from inside.

"My name is Jack Dawkins. I'm here with Greta, Ronan, and Sammy. We wanted to speak with you."

"Take a hike," Kieran said.

"You're sure this kid is worth rescuing?" Dawkins asked Greta. She frowned and opened her mouth to speak, but Dawkins stopped her with a raised hand. "Kidding! If you'd be so kind?" He stepped aside and gestured at the lock.

A moment later Dawkins pushed the door open.

"Hey!" Kieran yelped. "Where do you get off breaking into my room?" He was sitting on the bed. He was fully dressed except for his painted bite mask, which was on the desk next to a pile of open, empty wooden boxes. He took in the swords we were carrying, and for the first time since I'd met him, he looked afraid. "Wow," he said to Ogabe. "You're like the biggest person I've ever seen."

"There *are* bigger," Ogabe said, smiling. "But not many."

Kieran looked as tired as I felt, with big dark circles under his eyes. His eyes flicked over to Greta, Sammy, and me. "You're all disqualified. I'm going to be the winner. There's just one more test."

"That's why we're here," Dawkins said. "We have reason to believe you are not safe."

Kieran laughed. "Tell it to someone who cares, losers."

"Okay, we tried," Sammy said. "Now let's go."

And then I noticed Kieran's right hand: it flickered and glowed with a weird, red light. "You're wearing the Gauntlet!"

"Since I'm the last contestant, Vaughn gave me all the pieces." He raised his hand and flexed the fingers. I could see now that the red light came from the vein-like wires in the glass segments. They traced the shape of his hand in a glowing outline that seemed to flicker with its own pulse. "She says it's mine, so I put the pieces together and tried it on." The glass extended to just past his wrist, where a thick brass band held it in place.

"What does it do?" I asked.

"Wouldn't you like to know," Kieran said, sneering. He spread his fingers wide and the fingertips grew bright with light.

Dawkins readied his sword. "What's that you're doing?"

Kieran closed his hand into a fist. "I don't know," he said, slumping. "It just glows like that sometimes." He rested his hand on the rug. "Thing is super heavy, and, um, I don't know how to take it off."

"You can't take it off?" Sammy asked.

"The pieces won't come apart," Kieran said.

"Would you mind terribly if I looked more closely at it?" Dawkins said.

"Knock yourself out," Kieran said, standing and extending the Gauntlet.

Dawkins gently turned the glove over, saying, "These wire filaments channel energy from the wearer. See? This band around the wrist, it's some sort of conductor that feeds into the fingertips." He held the Glass Gauntlet between his own hands. "It's very warm, isn't it?"

"I can't feel that," Kieran said, frowning.

Dawkins frowned. "That can't be good. Listen, Kieran, this competition is not what it seems. Your host, the woman who calls herself Ms. Glass, is looking for . . . I don't know how to put this, exactly, but—"

"Rotten kids," Kieran said.

"You *knew* that?" I asked.

"You three dopes were the only ones who didn't," he said. "Vaughn recruited me after I got kicked out of an Outward Bound program in Idaho. That Elspeth girl? She just got out of juvie. She tried to poison a teacher when she was nine. I don't know where you three came from, but you were totally out of your depth."

"Still managed to beat you, though, didn't we?" Greta said.

"Greta," Dawkins said, "now is not the time for petty rivalries. Kieran, we can't stay here much longer. Agatha and Vaughn are not to be trusted. We are leaving, and we would like to take you with us for your own protection."

Kieran snorted. "I'm not going anywhere without my money."

"And we're not going anywhere without that Glass Gauntlet," Dawkins said. "I'm very sorry to have to force you, Kieran, but you leave me no choice. Ogabe?"

Ogabe reached down and grabbed the neck of Kieran's shirt. "Forgive me, son," he said, "but we'd like you to come with us." He pulled until Kieran was standing beside him.

Kieran pinwheeled his arms, swinging his fists through the air. "This is kidnapping!"

"Oh please," Dawkins said. "If you prefer, we could always cut off your hand. I can tell you from recent experience that it isn't much fun."

Kieran froze. "No, thank you."

"Suit yourself," Dawkins said. "Sammy, the iPad?"

"You stole that!" Kieran said.

"You dropped it," Sammy said. "I was going to give it back, but then . . . stuff happened." He messed around for a minute so that he could check the video feeds from downstairs. "Guys, I'm not getting anything from the cameras."

"That's not a promising sign," Dawkins said, sighing heavily.

"They figured out you dumbos were piggybacking." Kieran laughed. "So they turned the system off. Zing! Now you can't see them."

"Nor can they see us," Dawkins said. "Luckily, we've got an old-fashioned surveillance system." He bent down close to the four dogs and said, "Oh, War, Famine, Pestilence— and Debra!—have I told you lately what sweet pups you

180

are?" Their tails thumped the carpet. "How would you like to do a little exploring?"

Dawkins and the Dobermans slinked down the front staircase to the entry hall, with me, Greta, and Sammy hugging the wall behind them. Last to come was Ogabe, who held Kieran tight under one arm with a hand clamped over his mouth. Dawkins had removed the dogs' chain collars, and because of that they were weirdly quiet.

At the foot of the stairs, Dawkins whispered something to them, and the Dobermans split up. Two padded silently toward the central corridor, where Nestor had his security station. The dogs sniffed around a bit, then sat back and wagged their tails. "The corridor is empty," Dawkins whispered. The other two slinked across the black-and-white tile of the entry hall to the threshold of the sitting room, sniffed, and then backed away.

"Unfortunately, however," Dawkins whispered, "someone is in the sitting room."

"The back door is that way," Sammy said.

"There's another way out," I whispered. "Through the museum and that greenhouse."

Dawkins swept his hand toward the museum's double doors. "Lead the way."

Greta and I tiptoed across the middle of the room, glancing around nervously.

I froze.

The corridor was empty, all right—of *humans*.

Parked right in the middle was Agatha's robot. But it was facing away, toward the rear staircase, aiming something that looked an awful lot like a gun. Ready to fire on anyone who came down the back way.

I raised a finger to my lips and pointed, and Greta nodded. She crouched down in front of the museum door and got to work on the lock.

I'd never noticed before that every scrape and jiggle of a lock pick is crazy *loud*. But not so loud that anyone else noticed it before Greta had the door open.

All of us crept inside. At the last moment, Kieran thrashed in Ogabe's grip, but the big man just hugged him tightly to his chest. "Do not make us regret letting you keep your hand," he whispered after Greta had eased the door closed.

Dawkins led us to the aisle where the Damascene 'Scope had been hidden in its crate. The purple tarp was wadded up by the sliding door, and the cart with the crate was gone.

"The 'Scope is missing, but no matter. Once the Guard arrives, we'll track it down. Now, Ronan, how do we get out?"

"There's a mirror maze through here," Sammy said. He and I dragged open the big sliding door and held it until everyone was inside. Then we let it roll shut.

We were in complete and utter darkness. "There's a door on the other side of this room that connects to the greenhouse," I whispered.

"That's a bizarre architectural feature, wouldn't you say?" Dawkins asked. "Let me get out my lighter. Just a moment."

While he was digging around in his pocket, the door that had just rolled shut started to slide open again.

"It must be motorized," Sammy muttered.

A louder whirring drowned out the motor: the robot. It rolled forward into the mirror room. Even though the light was dim, I recognized what it was holding: a Tesla gun.

In the split-second space of a heartbeat, the dusty light in the room seemed to solidify, and I could see the violet threads of electricity slowly unfold from the gun's muzzle, could see everyone turning, surprised.

Sometimes the best weapon at hand, Dawkins had explained during Capture the Flag, *is your body itself. In such times, you must act fearlessly, without regard for injury. Hesitation softens the impact.* He'd paused, then added, *Though everything usually hurts a lot less if you take 'em out at the knees.*

My aim was perfect: I caught Dawkins, Greta, Sammy, and Ogabe in a flying tackle.

At the same moment, the air above us filled with lightning.

In one blazingly bright instant, the Tesla bolt struck the mirror, reflected across the room to another mirror, and back again, reflecting over and over at the speed of light, creating a crackling web of electricity that caught the robot's multilensed head dead center.

With a smoky explosion of white sparks, the LED eyebrows and the switches on its body went dark.

Abruptly, the mesh of light from the Tesla gun disappeared.

Dawkins, Greta, Sammy, Ogabe, and Kieran slid off me, and suddenly I could breathe again. The air stank of ozone, and the afterimages of the Tesla bolt made it difficult to see clearly.

"That," Dawkins said slowly, "was well done, Ronan." The Dobermans gathered around him and nosed his face. "I'm fine, you furry fools. Cut it out." He struck a flame from his lighter and held it aloft. In the faint glow, our reflections multiplied off the walls back and forth to infinity.

"This is no maze," Dawkins said, waving his other hand at the reflections. "It's the missing mirror box for the Damascene 'Scope. We're inside of it."

CHAPTER 19

A FISTFUL OF SOUL

In the dim light cast by the sparking robot and his Zippo lighter, Dawkins examined the walls around us and the angled center divider that split the room into two. "It appears to function perfectly."

"What does that mean, 'function perfectly'?" I asked. I could now see something I hadn't noticed before: the floor and ceiling were mirrored, too. It was hard to know where to look. A thousand dim versions of me stared out.

"These mirrors have been calibrated and oriented to reflect the beam from the Damascene 'Scope—or even a Tesla gun's stray bolt—onto a central focal point. Right about where that robot was parked, I'd reckon." Dawkins raised his lighter. "Which means dear Agatha is ready to *use* the 'Scope. That's why she needs our Verity Glasses."

"Then this room is dangerous to be in," Ogabe said. "We should leave as soon as possible." In his arms, Kieran struggled. "I will relax my grip if you promise to behave," Ogabe told him. Kieran's eyes above Ogabe's broad hand blinked, and his whole head nodded.

Suddenly all the dogs sat. "What's wrong?" Dawkins said, looking among them.

At the same moment, the room brightened—the doors to the greenhouse had been opened.

"They're obeying their master's voice," Agatha said, coming around the mirrored divider into the middle of the room. A silver dog whistle was in her hand, a chain dangling from it. And I'd thought it was just a stupid skeleton key necklace. "They likely remember the pain of their training."

Vaughn came in behind her, carrying Nestor's machine gun. She didn't bother to aim it at us, she just waved it and said, "Hello!"

"What became of the fat man and his crew?" Dawkins asked.

Agatha shrugged. "I kept zapping him until Vaughn and I could chain them all to the golf cart. We left them parked out front."

"That's not going to hold him for long," Dawkins said. "If you've got any smarts at all, you'll get out of here before his friends turn up."

"We'll be done by then," Agatha said. "Kieran?"

"Ow!" Ogabe yelped and dropped Kieran to the floor. There was blood between Ogabe's thumb and index finger, and red smeared across Kieran's face. "He *bit* me."

Kieran laughed, then leaped at Greta, pushing her against the mirrored wall with his left forearm.

"Hey!" I yelled, about to go after him, but Dawkins caught my shoulder.

Kieran's other hand, the one wearing the Glass Gauntlet, was spread wide against Greta's chest. The fingers were blindingly bright, like his whole hand was made of scarlet light. A pencil-thin red beam extended from each of the fingers and looped around her body, knotting together in a web of red light that had Greta's heart at its center.

Lux chirotheca, I thought. *Hand of light.* I knew without being told what those red beams would do—this Gauntlet was like the Eye of the Needle, that net of light that caught souls. I didn't want to see what would happen if he made a fist.

"I'm ready for my million bucks!" Kieran laughed. "Just give the order, Ms. Glass, and I'll do it!"

"Guys," Greta said, trembling, "I can't move."

"Not yet, Kieran," Agatha said. "Mr. Ogabe, your Verity Glass, please."

Ogabe reached under his shirt for a chain, then pulled it over his head and handed it to her. "You already trained the boy in the use of the Gauntlet?" he asked.

"Last night," Agatha said. "After we discovered the other kids had run away."

"Why'd you pretend?" I asked her. "Why be Blue and take the tests with us?"

"I needed to observe your behaviors up close," she said, pocketing the lens and walking back to Vaughn's side. "I needed to see who you *really* were, deep down."

"That's why I won," Kieran said. "She saw I was the best."

"The worst, you mean," Greta said.

"Same difference. Now I just have to pass the final test, using this." Kieran started to pinch his fingers shut, and the beams of light brightened as he drew them closer together.

Greta gasped in pain.

"Stop!" I shouted. "We'll do whatever you want—just let her go."

"That's enough, Kieran!" Agatha barked. "If you spoil her, you forfeit your reward."

"Yes, Ms. Glass." He relaxed his grip. "I wasn't really going to do it. Not yet."

Vaughn came around behind us with a length of chain, and she began to wrap it around our hands.

"Another magic trick?" Sammy asked.

"Old dog chain," Vaughn said, looping it around his wrists and snapping a padlock through it. "Tight enough for you?"

"If Kieran won your little contest, why do you need Greta?" Dawkins asked.

"I need *two* children, Jack," Agatha said. "First, one whose loyalty and morals are for sale, who will do anything for a price. That child will operate the Gauntlet for me—it works only for users who have yet to pass out of puberty."

Vaughn wrenched my arms behind me and coiled chain around my wrists.

"What does the Gauntlet do?" Dawkins asked. "I thought the Damascene 'Scope was the thing."

"You don't understand anything at all, do you, Jack?" Agatha laughed. "They are two *different* tools. The 'Scope alone allows purification of a soul. At least, that was the idea. But with the Gauntlet, a user can *pluck* a soul, place it within the 'Scope, and beam it into a new body. Which is why I needed the second child. I was going to use Elspeth, but Greta here is a much more appealing vessel." She tugged the flesh of her own forearm. "After two hundred years stuck in this tiny body, I will at last be able to grow up."

"And the soul in this 'appealing vessel,' as you call it— what happens to that?" Dawkins asked.

"Who cares?" Agatha shrugged. "But from what I understand, it's destroyed. Erased like it never existed. Poof!" She laughed.

Agatha and Vaughn sat the five of us in a row against the greenhouse wall while they set up the Damascene 'Scope on the massive wooden tripod. It was pointed through the open doors of the greenhouse into the heart of the mirror box like some kind of magical brass cannon.

Behind us, the Dobermans whined and scratched at the glass; the room was too small, so Agatha had shooed the dogs into the yard.

I was chained between Sammy on one side and Greta on the other. She squirmed against me, and I knew I should be trying to escape, too, but I was too upset to do anything. As soon as everything was ready with the Damascene 'Scope, Agatha was going to steal Greta's body and destroy Greta's soul. And Kieran was going to help her do it.

"The 'Scope malfunctioned that first time, back when we were children," Agatha explained to Dawkins while she peered through the eyepiece and made tiny adjustments. "And because of that, I came unstuck in time, my body frozen, never aging. Trapped by the Blood Guard's lousy science."

"All of this is just so you can grow up?" I muttered. "You're *sick*."

"Those who did this to me were the sick ones," Agatha replied. "And this is my chance to make things right."

All of a sudden I realized that I didn't care about Greta's being a Pure. Sure, deep down, I understood how her death would be capital-B Bad, that it could help bring about the end of the world and all that stuff the Blood Guard taught us. But all those reasons left me cold now. I didn't *feel* anything about any of that. What mattered was that she was my friend, maybe my best friend, and a terrible thing was going to happen to her unless I could stop it.

"Use me," I blurted. "For your vessel. Use me instead of Greta."

"No, thank you!" Agatha trilled. "Always the gallant one, aren't you, Ronan Truelove? Always trying to save

190

your girl. But you won't be able to do that here. My decision is made."

Greta turned and gave me a tiny smile. *Thanks,* she mouthed.

On the other side of her, Dawkins asked, "Our Verity Glasses are in that thing?"

"They were all I required to make it work properly," Agatha said, squinting into the eyepiece. She turned a brass crank, and the lens array moved incrementally. "Which is why I made sure to publicize my acquisition of the 'Scope far and wide. I wanted you and your friends to find out about it and bring me the final pieces."

"I searched for you for decades, you know," Dawkins said. "You and Spinks. You were the only family I ever had."

"You *abandoned* us," Agatha said, her eye still to the glass. "Vaughn, please have Kieran adjust his position one point two inches left."

Vaughn grabbed a tape measure and some string and disappeared into the mirror room. They'd left Kieran sitting inside, in the precise spot where the robot had been destroyed. Waiting to play his role in Greta's murder.

"I was captured," Dawkins said. "But I tried to find you two afterward."

"Liar," Agatha said. "You never raised a finger. Instead, you sent"—she spit—"the *Blood Guard.*" She said the name with such venom that I felt myself flinch. Was the Blood Guard so bad?

"They are good people," Dawkins said. "They offered to help when you and Spinks—"

"Do *not* say his name again!" Agatha snapped.

Dawkins sat up a little straighter. "He was my friend, too."

"I was not quite ten when they caught up to me and Spinks. The age you see before you now."

"What happened?" Dawkins asked quietly.

"The Blood Guard happened," Agatha said, sounding like Blue for the first time since we'd been in the hedge maze. "They said, 'We're here to save you.' They said, 'We can help you.' They said, 'We were sent by Jack Dawkins.' That was all we needed to hear to trust them.

"We were such little fools."

CHAPTER 20

A MOST UNFORTUNATE ACCIDENT

About a year after you disappeared, Spinks and me finally gave up our thieving ways. No more did we cut purses and lift wallets, no more did we do prospecting work for the toshers, those smelly men who combed the sewers for valuables. Instead, thanks to Saint Mary's, we'd stumbled onto a sweet gig.

We snuck in the back of the church one day to get warm, and old man Rumley took pity on us.

"I can't manage the bells no more," Rumley said, massaging his hands. "Go ahead—first this one, and then these two in order." There were lots of bell pulls, and lots of bells—later, Rumley showed us how to use them to play bits of song.

But that first time, it was just a simple call to Mass.

Spinks did the ringing mostly, being the sort who liked loud noises. The bells made a thunderous music that shook dust from the tower walls and vibrated deep in our bones.

In return for playing the bells, Rumley gave us two meals a day, a place to wash up, and a shed behind the rectory to sleep in.

We thought we'd gone to some kind of heaven.

It was a few months later that Rumley's curate, a woman named Teresa, sent us on an errand.

"Take this package to the vicar of Saint Pancras Old Church," she said, handing me something wrapped in brown paper that felt like a loaf of bread.

I picked at the twine around the paper and she slapped my hand away.

"Mind you don't open it," she said, scowling.

"Yes, mum," I said.

"Matthew"—that's what she called Spinks—"you'll wear an altar boy surplice so that nobody bothers you. People respect the cloth." The surplice was a long, white dressy thing that churchmen wore.

We hadn't been out and about in weeks, and we were kind of dizzy with the freedom of it, running and laughing and making people scowl. But then they would see Spinks in his gauzy white surplice, and they would either nod or avert their eyes. Back before, when Spinks and I were on the streets, it was like we were invisible: people didn't *want* to see us. Now they saw us and looked away out of respect.

"I'm a man of the cloth now, ain't I?" Spinks whispered,

his chin held high. "Even if someone felt their pocket get picked, they look back, see a man of the church."

"And me," I said, wishing I had some kind of church disguise of my own.

"People will look at us and be sure: those two holy children could never be thieves," Spinks said. "And then we just slip away in the crowd."

Suddenly I was worried. Spinks wanted to go back to our old way of living. "But why?" I said. "We got it good now."

"We can do better," Spinks said. "Do you see what I see?" He pointed to a fair that had set up in a square. "Opportunity."

People treat you different when they think you're holy, and we got let in free to a tent where there was a gorilla brought from Africa. The gorilla was black all over, even where it had no hair, and possessed of a face like a person's. Its eyes were wise and sad, all the wild gone away, probably the same time it got put in that iron cage.

"We should go," I told Spinks, looking at the package in my hands.

"What?" he asked. "We barely got here!"

"Something's wrong," I told him. "I want to go."

"Okay," he told me. "But not without I first get us a little something."

"Don't," I said, but he was already sidling off with that sideways step he used in crowds.

Turned out he was wrong; the altar boy garb didn't fool everyone. Or maybe he'd just got sloppy not having to steal for a living. Whatever the case, I heard the shout before I saw Spinks, squirming, the collar of his shirt held high by a bobby.

I should have just legged it straight back to the church. It was the smart play to make and what Spinks would have wanted me to do.

Two months earlier, I would have done. But instead, I ran straight at them, leaped onto the back of the bobby, and clawed at his eyes. My own eyes were filled with tears, and I couldn't see what I was doing. "Put him down!" I screamed.

I guess I got sloppy, too.

We were thrown into a stone room that, large as it was, wasn't big enough to hold all the people there. The smell was worse than the stink of the sewer, and the noise carried on all night and day. The only light that came in was from a row of tiny windows high up on the walls, where we could see the shadows of people's feet passing by.

"Your names?" asked a man on the other side of the ironwork gate to our cell.

Used to be we never gave our real names. I was Molly or Moira or Mary. But that was before. This time, I wanted Rumley to find us. "Agatha Glass," I told him.

Spinks looked shocked, but then leaned back and said, "Jack Dawkins."

The man's eyebrows rose. "I'll be back."

"I wonder if Rumley or Teresa will come," I asked. I didn't say what I was afraid of, that they would never forgive us. That they'd let us rot.

A few hours later, a gentleman in a velvet tailcoat and hat came and called out, "Agatha Glass?"

I looked up, but Spinks put his hand on my shoulder. "Easy," he said.

"And you gave your name as Dawkins, but you must be Matthew Spinks?"

By that time I'd heard enough. It had to be Rumley, come to rescue us. "That's me!" I cried, standing. "That's us!"

The turnkey opened the gate and we followed the gentleman down a hall past other holding cells, each packed with unfortunates like us, and up a curving stone staircase to a whitewashed corridor. He showed us into a clean room with a large wooden table and chairs.

"Agatha Glass," the man said. "And Matthew Spinks. You tried to steal that man's watch."

"I didn't mean anything, sir," Spinks started to say, but the man raised a hand to stop him.

"Making excuses will do no good. But what *will* do you good is helping me."

Spinks sat back, his face scrunched up with thought. "And if we don't help you?"

"No one knows you are here. You will spend years in this place." He lifted his hat and picked dust off the brim.

I thought of the gorilla in its cage. "Helping you sounds good," I said.

"Splendid! But first . . . you have no family at all, correct? No one who might miss you?" I thought of old Rumley and Teresa—I hoped they cared for us a little bit, but I couldn't believe they would miss us much, not after what we'd done.

We shook our heads.

He smiled, and it was a pretty thing to behold. His teeth were all still there, and his skin was as clear and clean as his clothes were well tailored. That was when I realized he hadn't been sent by old Rumley and Teresa after all.

"You two are exactly what we are looking for," he announced.

"Maybe you're not what we're looking for," Spinks said.

The man laughed. "I forgot the most important thing!" he said. "Someone has been searching for you these past months, someone who cares about you very much."

There was no one like that in the world, I knew, other than the boy sitting next to me. "Who?" I asked.

"His name is Jack Dawkins," the man announced.

I was overwhelmed by . . . I guess people call it *joy*. A chest-swelling, breath-catching, eye-watering kind of feeling, where I lost touch with what I was doing and just *felt* so much that it crowded out everything else. I can't remember how we left the jail, how our fine was paid or what Spinks and I said to each other, all I remember is how bright the room got and how happy I was, thinking, *He's alive Jack's alive Jack Dawkins is alive.*

The next day, we woke up in new quarters.

We'd each been given a room with a bed—a real bed, with a feather mattress, not straw—and a table with a pitcher of water and a bowl for washing. The walls were bright and clean, and everything smelled nice, which is to say it didn't smell at all for a change.

An old man woke us. "I'm the steward here at Saint Joseph's," he said.

"Is this a church?" I asked, because Saint-anything in a name usually means church.

He laughed. "Oh, no, dear girl. It's a medical college."

He took us to a room for breakfast—mush with milk, bread with butter, and coffee with sugar if we wanted it. While we ate, the old man went away and another man came in.

"Good morning!" he said. "I am Dr. Torqué, the lead researcher here at Saint Joseph's." He was bald, but had a thick beard and glasses, and he showed us around after breakfast.

"You are in a residency wing of the medical college," he said, herding us from the small dining room down a corridor to a pair of double doors.

He showed us a glove made of glass. I made the mistake of picking it up.

"Oh no, little girl," said Dr. Torqué. "That is for your friend's experiment, not yours." He took it from me and had Spinks try it on. "It fits beautifully!"

"It's too heavy to pick a pocket with," Spinks said.

Dr. Torqué laughed. "You'll be picking something far more valuable with that!" He replaced the glove and then led us down the hall. "And this is the room in which you will help us with our work, little girl."

We were in the topmost row of a U-shaped theater. Below, in the center of the room, was a five-foot-by-five-foot black box. Aimed directly at it was a fat brass pipe, one end of which extended through a black glass panel.

"That," he said, pointing, "is the Damascene Achromatic Animascope, which we will use on you, Agatha," and then he went on to describe how it worked, but I had stopped listening a long time before, when I realized he wasn't taking us to see Jack.

"Where's Jack?" I asked, interrupting.

He spluttered to a stop. "I'm sorry, little girl. Jack who?"

"Dawkins," I said. "Jack Dawkins. Our friend. He sent you to find us."

Dr. Torqué shook his big bald head. "Oh, no, I do not know this Dr. Dawkins."

"He's not a doctor," I said. "He's a boy."

"Then that explains it!" He laughed. "I tell you what. After we finish our testing here in three days, you can go find your friend. Okay?"

Without waiting for an answer, Dr. Torqué began talking again. I didn't understand much of what he was saying, but I got a few things. Spinks and I were part of different experiments. Spinks had to do something using that glass glove, but all I had to do was sit in a chair and get "showered in radiance" from the brass pipe. The light from this device, he told me, would make me *good*. I would be like an angel on earth.

"Doesn't that sound wonderful?" he said.

"No," Spinks replied. "Angels are boring." And we both snickered.

"Perfect." Dr. Torqué seemed delighted by our laughter. "You are the ideal specimens!"

Later that day, a woman came to interview us. She wanted us to tell her every bad thing we'd ever done. Stole bread? Lots of times. Snatched purses? Tons. How many? More than in all the stores on the high street, Spinks said.

We just made up things, whatever we thought she wanted to hear. The more we talked, the more outrageous we got. We never killed anyone, but when she asked, "Have you ever *murdered* a person?" we couldn't stop ourselves lying.

"Oh, gobs of people," Spinks said. "You just get a rock and *bam*!"

On the second morning, Dr. Torqué came and led Spinks out, leaving me in my room.

He didn't come back by dinnertime, though the old man brought me a tray of stewed beef and bread. After, when I banged on my locked door, he came and took the tray away.

"Where's my friend?" I asked.

"I'm sorry, miss," the old man said. And then he left, turning the key in the lock.

I don't know how long I banged on the door of my cell that night. For hours I shouted, screaming until I was so hoarse that it hurt to make any sound at all.

When the door finally opened in the morning, Dr. Torqué and the woman stared at me in shock.

"What happened to your hands?" the woman asked.

I looked down. I had beat them bloody against the door in the dark. No wonder they hurt. "Sorry," I said, and went to wash up at the basin.

"Never mind that," the doctor said. "We are ready for you! It is time to undergo the process!"

"Where is Spinks?" I asked. And when they looked confused, I said, "My friend. The boy who was here with me?"

"Oh!" Dr. Torqué laughed. "He's fine! He performed his experiment with the Gauntlet yesterday, and is now recuperating. You can join him afterward."

"Really?" I said, relieved. "Okay. Let's get this over with."

Back then, the Damascene 'Scope was a primitive device. The mirror box was a five-foot square cube with a wooden chair in the center. I was seated and my wrists and ankles belted into place, while all around me men in white coats polished the mirrors that covered the inside of the box.

"What's going to happen?" I asked.

Dr. Torqué patted my hand and said, "Just a little bit of light will shine on you. That's all."

A silence fell as every light in the room was extinguished.

Finally, a voice whispered, "The Pure is in position on the other side of the window!" and someone opened a shutter.

And in a flash, all the love and hope and joy I carried in my heart shriveled away into nothing.

Afterward, someone must have carried me to my cell. The woman who came to wake me that evening told me I had thrashed against my bonds until I'd fallen unconscious.

"That so?" I asked. "I feel okay now." In fact, I felt better than I ever had. I was *angry*, but that wasn't a bad thing. The anger made it easier to know who I had to hurt. *Dr. Torqué. This woman. All of the doctors at Saint Joseph's. The gentleman with the top hat. Jack Dawkins.* I smiled at her.

She escorted me to the little dining room down the hall. Dr. Torqué sat at the head of the table. There was roast beef carved up on a platter, and mashed potatoes and bread. But I wasn't hungry.

"How are you feeling?" he asked.

At the sight of him, I was furious to a degree I'd never felt before, my muscles so rigid that I had to struggle not to make claws of my hands. "Where is Spinks?"

"I'm afraid he didn't make it," Dr. Torqué said. "During his experiment, something went awry with the Gauntlet, and he, um, tragically perished."

Whatever small glimmer of light inside me that I'd clung to went out, and I felt as cold and alone as I ever have.

"What did you do to him?" I asked, picking up a butter knife to look at my reflection. I looked the same as ever on the outside.

"It was a most unfortunate accident. We are still learning, you see, still calibrating our instruments," Dr. Torqué said, slathering butter on a roll. "But we achieved perfection with your experiment, my dear—*you* are a success."

I knew I'd suffered an unfortunate accident, too, but I couldn't put my finger on precisely what had happened. "I do *feel* different," I said, changing my grip on the knife. "But I don't know why."

"What you feel," Dr. Torqué said, spreading his arms wide, "is the absence of the evil that once blackened your soul!"

"No," I said, "I don't think that's it."

And then I leaped across the table with the butter knife and stabbed him through his fat, dark heart.

CHAPTER 21

A MOMENTARY FLASH OF BRILLIANCE

"Those men were cast out of the Guard," Dawkins said, staring at the floor of the greenhouse. "They were pseudoscientists who believed they could harness the light of the Pure we guard and use it to make the world a better place."

Agatha snorted. "A better place! They lured an unwitting Pure—I never learned who he or she was—into the room behind the shutter, and then they burned me with the Pure's radiance." She narrowed her eyes at Dawkins. "It *burned*, Jack."

"I thought the Blood Guard were supposed to be the good guys," I said.

"Do good guys experiment on children?" Agatha snapped. "Those *good guys* came after us thanks to Jack Dawkins."

"I never asked them to do *that*," Dawkins exclaimed. "I was just a kid myself. I needed help finding you, and my friend Jenks put out the word."

"So the Damascene 'Scope was supposed to make you good, but it malfunctioned and made you evil?" I asked, blinking. It had gotten hotter while she'd talked, and now sweat was running into my eyes.

"Evil?" Agatha said, tilting her face to the sun and shutting her eyes. "Who can really say what *evil* is?"

"It's evil not to give us a drink of water," Sammy said. "I'm dying of thirst here."

"Killing a man with a butter knife?" Greta said, squirming against the wall. "I'd say that pretty much falls under the heading of evil."

Agatha grinned. It was hard to remember, looking at her, that she wasn't really a skinny little nine-year-old. "Perhaps! Torqué had no idea what he was doing, but I swore, I'd reconstruct the device one day—and this time, it would work perfectly." She closed the hatch on the outside of the 'Scope and ran a rag over the brass, polishing it so that it shone in the sunlight.

"And did you rebuild that glass glove, too?" Dawkins asked.

"No, *that* I stole." Agatha peered through the eyepiece. "I burned down Saint Joseph's, but I kept the Gauntlet. It killed Spinks, and I hated it, but I was poor and thought I might be able to sell it. But no one ever wanted to buy it."

"But it's still untested!" Dawkins struggled against the chains linking us all. "It didn't work then, and because of that, Spinks died. What makes you think it's going to work any better now, two hundred years later?"

"According to Torqué's notes, the Gauntlet worked perfectly. Spinks died afterward, in an unfortunate side effect." Agatha turned a lever, and a shutter or something inside the 'Scope must have opened up, because I could see through the door that the mirror room was filling with light, becoming even brighter than the greenhouse.

"That is *blinding*," Sammy said, turning his face away.

"A few final calibrations, a few last instructions for Kieran," Agatha said, "and we will be ready!" She walked away into the searing glare.

The moment she was gone, Greta stood up, the chain a shiny pile behind her. "I thought she'd never leave."

"Save yourself, Greta," Dawkins said. "It's your body she's after. She can't do this insane soul transfer if you're not here. Run."

"No way," Greta said, crouching down to get at Dawkins' hands. "We're in this together."

Greta was in front of Dawkins, with her back to the house. That's why neither of them saw the shadow appear in the light-filled doorway.

But Sammy and I did: Kieran, strolling into the greenhouse to take his position, staring down at the glowing Glass Gauntlet on his hand while he flexed it open and closed. He looked up and saw Greta unlocking Dawkins.

With a strangled cry, he closed the Gauntlet into a fist and ran at her.

Our training took over. Sammy twisted and tripped Kieran as he ran, I caught him with my feet against his chest, then rolled him right over Greta and into the greenhouse pane above her.

He smacked it headfirst. And then my legs gave out and he fell on top of us.

A moment later he was lifted off—by Dawkins, who set Kieran on the floor, grabbed Agatha's polishing rag off the 'Scope, and stuffed it into Kieran's mouth. "Bite on this for a change."

By that time, Greta had released Ogabe, who helped me and Sammy to our feet. "Greta will free you," Ogabe whispered, "while we stand guard." He and Dawkins moved to either side of the doorway, out of sight of anyone inside.

Sammy and I stared out at the back lawn, our hands behind us, while Greta unlocked our cuffs.

"Check it out," Sammy whispered. "We're casting a shadow."

"Of course," Greta said, fiddling with my chains. "It's almost noon, and the sun's right overhead."

"Not from the sun," he said.

He was right. Whatever the Damascene 'Scope was doing, the light it beamed into the mirror room reflected and multiplied and burned so brightly that it somehow blazed stronger than the sunlight. Our shadows were *behind* us, not under us, and they stretched through the glass of the greenhouse and across the grass.

My chains fell away and I looked back, raising my hands to cover my eyes. "Is it supposed to get that bright?"

Greta turned, too, facing the 'Scope straight-on. "You think it's malfunctioning again?" She seemed almost haloed in light, and then—

There was a brief, dazzling flash.

"What just happened?" Sammy asked, blinking.

"Something blew up inside, maybe?" I said, wiping the sweat from my face.

From inside the house came a shriek, and Vaughn ran out, wraparound sunglasses on her face. "What have you done?" she cried. She stopped in front of the 'Scope, the gun forgotten in her hands. "Kieran? Get up. Why are you children unlocked?"

Ogabe stepped up behind her and wrenched the gun away. "They're not the only ones."

"Greta, Sammy," Dawkins said, "help Ogabe chain up our Ms. Vaughn. Ronan, come with me."

I followed him inside, and he pulled the doors shut, cutting off the light and plunging the mirror room into a cool darkness. While our eyes adjusted, he flipped open his lighter and struck a flame. His face in the dim light was more serious than I'd ever seen.

"I need you to take Greta to safety. Head for that garage, and if you can't find a vehicle, make for the back wall of the estate. Bring the dogs. If anyone tries to mess with you, they'll have the Four Horsemen to deal with."

"But what about the 'Scope and the Glass Gauntlet?"

"Our problem. Yours is keeping Greta away from Agatha and the Damascene 'Scope. More than Greta's life is riding on it."

"I understand," I said, nodding. This, at least, I could do. I wouldn't have to come up with some reason to protect Greta—she already knew that Agatha wanted to steal her body. This time, she'd listen. "And once we get out of here, where should we go?"

As we circled the room's mirrored divider into the central chamber, Dawkins said, "I don't know, Ronan. You'll have to figure that part out yourself. Someplace safe, someplace unexpected. We can always get back into contact through KoalaKlub."

"Okay," I said. Our eyes had fully adjusted, and now I could see Dawkins. He was looking the other way, toward the museum. "You can count on me. I'll go right now."

"What is that?" he asked.

In the dark ahead of us was a pale shape.

Dawkins walked toward the sliding door, the Zippo held aloft. As we got closer, I was able to make out a shadowy figure slumped unconscious in a chair.

Agatha.

CHAPTER 22

AGATHA UNDONE

"Let's get some light in here," Dawkins said. "Can you open that door?"

I started to pull it open when suddenly the motor engaged, and the door began sliding aside all by itself. Weak light from within the museum filled the room, casting multiplied reflections of Dawkins in the walls, floor, and ceiling tending to dozens of Agathas.

"She's alive," he said, taking her from the chair and laying her out on the floor. "But unconscious."

"What happened?"

"Your guess is as good as mine, Ronan," he said, shaking his head. "Heat stroke? Guilty conscience? Embarrassment?"

Just then a creepily familiar voice boomed out from the museum.

"Little girl?" Steiner called. "Is this where you've come to hide?" Footsteps and shuffling noises echoed across the big room. "Three and Four, search that row of telescopes over there. One and I will take this row of magical paraphernalia."

"Opening the door to the greenhouse will make this room light up like a solar flare," Dawkins whispered.

"We can close *this* one," I whispered, pointing to the door of the museum.

"Too much noise." The purple tarp that had covered the 'Scope's crate was still wadded up by the entrance. Dawkins picked it up and carried it inside, handing it to me. "We'll hide under this."

"You don't think they'll see us?"

"Of course they'll see us," he whispered. "But what's one more weird purple lumpy thing in a museum full of weird lumpy things? Get down."

I crouched next to Agatha, and from the other side, Dawkins pulled the tarp over us like a bedsheet. The last thing he said was "*Shh*."

The sound of two people's heels against the tile grew louder as they came to the mirror room's open doorway. One of the agents paused. I imagined him unslinging a Tesla rifle, aiming it at the purple tarp, and pulling the trigger.

The bolt would hit us any moment now.

Except instead, the footsteps started again, the sound getting softer and softer as the agent wandered farther down the aisle.

Dawkins slid the tarp away and handed me the Zippo, then cradled Agatha in his arms.

I must have stared, because he whispered, "What? I can't just leave her. Besides, she's the only one who understands how the Gauntlet and 'Scope work."

I led the way back around the mirror room's divider to the greenhouse. For a split second as I opened the doors, the mirror room dazzled with light. I prayed Steiner and his agents wouldn't notice, but I knew deep down that they would.

Sammy appeared next to us holding the end of the long chain that was now locked around Vaughn. "To lock the doors," he said, and the two of us knotted it tight through the handles.

When we finished, Greta was there, her hand extended. Sitting on her open palm were two Verity Glasses, mine in its tarnished silver frame, and another, set in a simple gold band of metal. "Ogabe already took his."

I draped the chain back around my neck and felt a strange relief as its cool weight settled against my chest. It was back where it belonged.

"Would you mind holding on to that for me?" Dawkins asked, shifting Agatha in his arms. "My hands are kind of full at the moment."

"What happened to Agatha Glass?" Ogabe asked.

"Haven't the foggiest," Dawkins replied. "We found her in there, out cold."

"She's awake now," Greta said, pointing.

Agatha stared up at Dawkins with her enormous blue eyes and blinked, then rolled them and looked at each of us. She coughed.

"We can tie her up later," Dawkins said. "Right now, we need to make double time out of here. Steiner and his agents are inside the museum."

Just then, the chained doors to the mirror room rattled.

"Correction: they're inside the mirror room and coming this way. Let's go."

"What should we do about those two?" Ogabe asked, gesturing.

Kieran was still lying tied up on the floor, feverish and moaning and completely out of it. He didn't look good. Vaughn was chained next to the door, glaring at us.

"They can sweat it out in here," Dawkins said, toeing open the glass door to the outside.

"No!" Agatha croaked. I barely heard her, but all of us stopped moving.

Dawkins shook his head. "Sorry, but I'm not inclined to honor the wishes of vicious imps."

Someone banged on the chained doors again. They swelled outward with a metallic groan, but the chain held.

"Not much time," Ogabe said, grabbing our weapons from the corner.

"The *boy*," Agatha whispered. "Bring him."

"Do you really think we're going to drag your little servant with us so that you can retrieve the Gauntlet?" Dawkins asked.

"Fool!" Agatha rolled her eyes, and for a half second she reminded me of the girl named Blue who I'd believed was a kid. "Don't care 'bout that!" she rasped, and even though her voice was faint, I could hear her exasperation. "But Kieran—the Gauntlet will kill him."

Outside, the dogs bounded happily around us until Dawkins calmed them with a low whistle. He squinted at the faraway building and said, "No, that won't do at all," and then galloped toward the corner of the house. Only once we'd passed the back door and gone around the corner of the kitchen did he pause.

"Aren't we going to the garage?" Greta asked.

"That route would take too long," Dawkins said. "Steiner and his goons need only take a gander out the greenhouse, and they'd see us crossing that great expanse of grass." He shifted Agatha in his arms and said, "How does such a tiny slip of a girl weigh so much?"

"Agatha wasn't lying," Ogabe said. "This boy feels quite sick."

We'd all cooled off in the breeze outside the greenhouse. Not Kieran. If anything, he looked even sweatier against Ogabe's shoulder.

"I don't know where to go," I said. "They're in the house, so we can't get to the tunnels. And on foot we're at least fifteen minutes from anywhere."

"The cart!" Agatha croaked. "Out front."

"She's right," Greta said. "Steiner and his goons are in the museum, looking for us on the back lawn. That means the golf cart Agatha and Vaughn chained them to is—"

Dawkins had already taken off, heading toward the front of the house. "What are you waiting for?" he called back. "Come *on*!"

The golf cart looked like it had gone through a war. The railings had been wrenched out in some places, and in others they had melted into little puddles of now-cooled-again steel. The windshield was just a jaggedy line of broken glass.

"Quite the stylish ride," Dawkins said, sliding into the passenger seat.

Greta, Sammy, and I climbed into the space where the backseat had been. Ogabe laid Kieran in the little cargo area behind us, then climbed behind the wheel and stomped on the accelerator.

Golf carts, it turns out, don't go very fast. But at least their electric motors are quiet.

We whirred away from the front of the house, around the black fountain, and out onto the main drive, the four Dobermans running alongside.

"We are completely exposed on this road," Ogabe said. "And at this speed, it will be at least five to ten minutes before we're out of sight of that house."

"And they have an SUV," Greta said, looking behind us. She reached over to Kieran, took the gag from his mouth, and wiped his face with the clean end of it. "He's not doing so great."

"I don't get it," I said. "He signs up for a plan to kill

you, and now you're trying to take care of him?"

"That wasn't *his* idea. I mean, I don't *like* him, but I don't want him to *die*." Greta shrugged. "He's just a mixed-up kid who Agatha exploited. He's here for the money, that's all."

"Greta is right," Dawkins said. "It's this evil monkey's doing. Speaking of which"—he jostled Agatha—"any helpful suggestions of where we might hide, evil monkey?" But she'd fallen unconscious again.

"The maze," Sammy said, pointing to the brown smudge on our left. "It's a lot closer than the gate, and I can use Kieran's iPad to close the hedges around the center so no one can get in."

"A splendid suggestion, Sammy," Dawkins said, just as Ogabe cranked the wheel of the cart hard left, toward a stone pathway that wound across the grass.

The maze was just as disturbing up close the third time around. Ogabe steered the cart down the clear aisle between the dead hedges, straight to the center. We climbed out onto the grass and looked back toward the faraway black smudge of the house. Now that there was something between us and Steiner, I almost felt safe.

Sammy pulled out Kieran's iPad and tapped at it, and suddenly the screen filled with an image of a white maze on a black background.

"Sammy," Ogabe said, "let's be careful. Once those hedges start moving around, it will be clear someone's in here."

"Getting everything ready just in case we need to close it up," Sammy said.

While the Dobermans chased each other around the base of the hill, Dawkins laid Agatha out on the grass. Her eyes were open again.

"I've no idea why you were helpful just now," Dawkins said, "but that's no matter. I'm not going to feel safe unless you are tied up."

"I understand," Agatha said.

"Rope would be better, but this will do in a pinch." He dragged over the coiled water hose and looped it tightly around Agatha again and again, binding her arms to her sides, and finally weaving the nozzle through the loops and yanking it tight. "Ronan, can you open the tap, please?"

I turned the knob and the hose swelled with water, the loops creaking and tightening until Agatha coughed.

"Tight enough for you?" Dawkins asked, nodding. "Good."

"Jack," Ogabe called. "The boy is dying. I can barely feel a pulse."

Dawkins glanced at Kieran, then back at Agatha. He looked as angry as I've ever seen him. "You did this," he said and then handed me the short sword I'd had earlier. "Ronan, watch her. If she misbehaves, scratch her." He stalked away.

"The hose," Agatha said, struggling. The hose was so tight around her that she couldn't take a deep breath. "The water."

"Sorry," I told her. "It looks pretty snug, but I can't do anything about that."

"On the *Gauntlet*," she said. "Electric connections. Short out. In water." Her eyes narrowed at me. "Electromagnets. Short them out. *Dummy*."

Suddenly I understood what she was saying. "Sorry about this!" I said, and then I yanked on the nozzle of the hose and dragged it—and Agatha—along the grass to where Dawkins, Ogabe, Sammy, and Greta were huddled over Kieran.

"Guys!" I shouted. "Stand back!" I squeezed the trigger.

The water sprayed wide, soaking everyone. Greta, Sammy, and Ogabe just sat there, too surprised to move, but Dawkins leaped out of the way.

He grabbed the spray nozzle from me and snarled, "What are you doing?"

"Jack," Greta said. "Look."

He glanced back. "Well, what do you know."

The Glass Gauntlet had come apart around Kieran's hand, sparks chasing each other through the wiring in the glass and then dimming.

Greta reached out and snapped the brass cuff off Kieran's wrist, then pushed the glass components into the center of the rag that had been in his mouth. She tied up the corners into a little bundle, the pieces clinking together like my mom's china.

"Ronan, well done," Dawkins said.

"It was Agatha's idea," I said. "Seemed to make sense."

Squirting the water from the hose had eased the pressure

219

around Agatha's middle. She was breathing easier now. "He's all right?" she asked.

I looked at Kieran. "He still looks pretty awful, but the Gauntlet is off."

"Good," she said. "Normally it doesn't release the user until death. That's what killed Spinks."

Dawkins squinted down at her, and then over at Kieran again. "Why are you being so helpful all of a sudden?"

"I don't know," Agatha said, frowning. "Something's different. I feel *good*."

Good. I thought about Greta haloed in sunshine behind the lens array. That bright flash in the greenhouse. "What happened to you in the mirror room?" I asked. "Do you remember?"

"I was in the subject's chair and sent Vaughn to the greenhouse to get a light reading, and then . . ." She swallowed.

"And then *what*?" Dawkins asked. "You were overcome by your own mean spirit?"

"The world burned away," she said. "Everything everywhere became bright, and warm, and beautiful, and I became part of it, and it became part of me." Agatha laughed. "It was a miracle."

"Doesn't sound like a miracle to me," Dawkins said. "More like delusion."

"No," Agatha said, seeming almost to talk to herself, "the Damascene 'Scope *changed* me."

"*Ha!*" Dawkins said. "You think you can con us so

easily? No way. We've seen the real you."

"But how?" Agatha went on, ignoring him. "The lenscraft is the best that modern science can achieve, but the 'Scope shouldn't work unless a Pure is in the proper position, one whose reflected light can be gathered and transmitted by the device."

I swallowed. Greta had been standing behind the 'Scope, undoing my chains.

"But what about the Glass Gauntlet?" I asked, yanking on the hose and tightening the coils again. "Don't you need Kieran to use it to pull out a soul, put it into the 'Scope, and beam it at you?"

"That's the 'Scope's *second* setting," Agatha quietly said. "But the first setting doesn't use the Gauntlet at all. It erases the nastiness from people's souls by using the magnified radiance of a Pure—"

"We know the theory," Dawkins growled.

I sat down next to her on the grass. Had Greta's . . . *radiance* burned away all the bad in Agatha, transforming her into a sweet nine-year-old girl? The same girl Dawkins had known back in London in the 1830s?

"Oh, dear boy!" Agatha said. "You did it by accident, didn't you? There is only one explanation for this: you have a Pure with you!"

"No," I said. "We don't have a Pure with us at all!"

"You're a poor liar, Ronan Truelove," Agatha said, smiling again. She looked like the happiest crazy person in the world. "Is it Samuel? Or the girl?"

"A Pure?" Dawkins asked, frowning. "Why ever would you think that?"

"Because the Damascene 'Scope *works*, Jack," Agatha said. "And I'm the living proof of it. I am a changed woman," she said, glancing down at herself. "Girl. I don't know what I am anymore. But I do know that I am *good*. And I want to make up for the things I've done wrong."

"You'll forgive me if I don't believe you." Dawkins sounded sarcastic, but his face looked—I don't know, *hopeful*, maybe. He stared at Agatha, his mouth open, obviously thinking.

Could a person be changed like that, flipped like a coin from one side to the other—from good to evil and back again? I thought of my dad, who I'd believed was a good guy until I learned the opposite was true. But that was about me and my perceptions. This was about who Agatha was deep down, who she'd always been.

"I do," I said. "I believe her."

"Ronan," Dawkins said, pulling me away to where the hose was attached to its spigot.

"Greta was behind the 'Scope," I whispered to Dawkins, "and the light—it went through the 'Scope and into the mirror room and hit Agatha. She really is different."

"Don't let her fool you, Ronan," Dawkins said. "You want to think the best of people, and I admire that, but this twisted urchin is not to be trusted."

"She's been helping us—"

"Self-preservation," Dawkins said.

"You think she just got lucky and guessed we have a Pure with us? No, Jack—she *knows* what Greta is, because the Damascene 'Scope wouldn't work otherwise."

"I'd like that to be true." He stared at Agatha for a long moment, and then groaned in frustration. "It's a very convincing argument, Ronan. Nonetheless, it would be reckless to free her."

Dawkins once told me that a Blood Guard faces a thousand tiny tests, little decisions that don't appear to matter much. But putting it that way makes it sound easy, like it's always obvious what's right and what's wrong. It's only when the right thing to do *isn't* obvious that you are truly tested.

"Reckless, maybe," I said. "But probably the right thing to do."

Dawkins stared into my eyes, like he was taking measure of me in a new way. Then he smacked my arm. "Okay, Ronan. Go and untie her. I'll turn off the water."

I'd just finished freeing her when Sammy called out, "Guys? Something weird is happening." He swiped at the iPad, frustrated. "I'm locked out again."

I walked over, the spray nozzle in my hand.

Around us, the maze was rewriting itself, the pathway we'd taken closing up as, one by one, the hedge rows noisily ratcheted back into place. The brown walls shivered around until they formed a solid wall.

"Who's doing this?" Dawkins asked Agatha at the same time as, on Sammy's screen, another aisle opened up.

"Behind us," Sammy said. "They're coming in behind us!"

Ogabe, Dawkins, Greta, and I watched as a line of seven dark-suited figures approached down a new aisle at the back of the maze. They might have looked like they'd just gone for a stroll in the sunshine, except for the swords and Tesla rifles they carried.

"I'm guessing they spotted us coming here on the cart," Dawkins said, unsheathing his saber.

Agatha shook off the last loop of hose and went to Sammy. "Give me that. We have to reboot the system. Now."

"Who let you out?" he asked.

She took the iPad from him and began typing so fast her hands were a blur.

Ogabe raised his blade and said, "Greta, stick close to Sammy and . . . Agatha?"

"I'll explain later," Dawkins said. He whistled softly and the Dobermans ran to him.

On one end of the line of seven people was a beautiful black woman. She had her left arm raised and was weaving a complicated pattern in the air with her fingers. A Bend Sinister Hand, controlling the five agents who served her.

On the other end of the line of agents was a tall, clean-shaven man wearing a dark natty suit with a white shirt and tie, shiny shoes, and a pocket handkerchief. He looked like some sort of smug big shot, like a stockbroker or a politician. I almost didn't recognize him.

But then he spread his arms wide and said, "Evelyn! Son! I've come for you."

CHAPTER 23

EVERYONE GETS PRETTY STEAMED

My dad.

He was acting like this was some sort of happy reunion, like I'd invited him to come meet me here. I mean, I *had* invited him—but as a *ploy*, not because I really wanted to see him. We were supposed to have been long gone by now.

I froze, ashamed and confused about what I should say or do, but then I remembered what my mom had told me: Being a Blood Guard wasn't about *me*. It was about something bigger. It was about protecting Greta, about saving Flavia.

I knew what I had to do.

I blasted him in the face with the water hose.

He didn't make a sound as he was thrown backward. And I didn't have time to watch him get up, because the rest of his team broke into a run.

The Hand and three of her agents went after my friends, but the other two came straight for me.

I knocked the first aside with a shot of water to the belly, then directed the stream at his bald friend. The man spluttered and slid down the hill a few steps, fighting the column of water and trying to draw his sword.

At the same time, I caught sight of the first guy aiming his Tesla gun and firing.

I snapped the stream from my hose right across the path of the Tesla bolt.

The light beam hit the water and—*poof*—vaporized it.

Instantly, giant clouds of crackling, hissing steam billowed out, and the entire clearing filled with superheated fog. I could no longer see the Bend Sinister, the Blood Guard, or anything else. But I kept my finger on the trigger, kept sweeping the water back and forth like some kind of human lawn sprinkler.

"Greta!" I shouted.

From the fog came sounds of mayhem: a shimmery scraping of swords exiting scabbards, a wild tramping of feet. I heard Dawkins shout out, "Strong work, Ronan!" followed by a flurry of grunts and punches, and then a polite, "*I'll* take that, thank you very much." From farther away, Ogabe roared, and there was the *smack* of bodies striking bodies.

"Ronan!" Agatha called from behind me. "Get to the tree!"

I tried to follow the hose back uphill, but I'd dragged it around so much that it no longer went in a straight line.

Directly in front of me another flicker of purple light burst—a Tesla bolt lost in the steam.

I aimed straight at it. A satisfying hiss and crackle came from the fog, along with a frustrated shout.

I realized—too late—that to find me, the Bend Sinister had only to follow the stream of water.

A shadowy figure loomed out of the mist, raising its sword arm high.

I froze.

Suddenly Dawkins materialized from the fog, leaping between us and blocking the downward chop with his own blade.

Behind me, a Tesla gun fired off again and again. Crackling bolts of purple lightning sizzled over my head.

They can't see me, I reassured myself. *They're shooting wild.*

Greta shouted, "This way!"

I followed her voice uphill, coiling the hose around my arm and dragging it behind me. The mist was changing, going from steamy white to a dirty brown tinged with orange light.

Because the dead bushes of the hedge maze were on fire.

I had almost reached the stumpy tree—I could see the dark shadow of it rising from the grass ahead of me—when the pressure in the hose decreased. I stopped, squeezed the nozzle, and watched my jet of water dribble into nothing.

Then the hose yanked tight, cinching around my arm and jerking me backward.

I started sliding across the slope. Through the smoke, I could see a dark figure hauling on the hose, pulling it hand over hand. And beside him, plunged point-first into the ground, was a big saber. Waiting for me.

"Help," I croaked.

Then Greta came bursting out of the smoke and fog, shouting, "Hey, mister!"

The Bend Sinister agent dropped the hose and reached for his saber, but too late: before the man could swing again, four Doberman-shaped shadows flowed from out of the smoke and dragged him away. Greta plucked the saber out of the ground and tossed it to me pommel-first.

I caught it with my left hand. "Thanks!"

"No problem," Greta said, whistling the Dobermans back to her. She cranked the wheel on the spigot, and the water pressure in the hose surged. "Come on already."

We found Sammy and Ogabe by the little tree, Kieran laid out unconscious between them. Agatha hovered behind, her pale hair and white skin making her look like a soot-covered ghost.

"Fine work with that hose, Ronan," Dawkins said, appearing out of the smoke with a sword in each hand. "Bought us some time."

"It wasn't exactly—"

"I know the steam was an accident, but accidents favor the brave." Dawkins pointed his sword at Agatha. "Can you open that tunnel?"

Agatha frowned. "It's locked from below."

"That's what I was afraid of. Sammy, do you have control of the maze again?"

"Yeah," Sammy said. "Agatha rebooted the system."

"Then open us a path out of here," Dawkins said. "Ogabe will carry Kieran and lead. I'll create distractions while the rest of you get clear."

I started to put down the hose, but Dawkins stopped me.

"Why discard something that's served you so well? A sword is absolutely no defense against water." He smiled. "Besides, you're going to need that."

"Why?" I asked.

"The maze is on fire. Surely you've noticed." He took a step forward into the smoke and then turned back. "Give a holler if you run into serious trouble."

"What should I holler?" I asked.

"Oh, I don't know. *Pizza!* always gets my attention."

And then he was gone.

Down the hill on the far side of the clearing, we stopped in front of the innermost maze wall.

We couldn't see the hedges anymore; they were a wall of flames rising twenty feet high into the air. The heat was so intense that even breathing was difficult.

Sammy pressed his fingers against the iPad, and with an ear-piercing shriek of gears and motors, the burning bushes in front of us parted like fiery curtains. He did it again and the next hedge did the same, and then the one after that, until there was an alley through seven layers of the maze like an aisle cutting through rows of tall bookshelves in a library. But the eighth, most faraway bunch of hedges didn't move at all.

I opened the nozzle and sprayed down the flames to either side, until our path was lined by blackened hedges.

"It's stuck," Sammy said.

"I'll take care of getting us through there," Ogabe said, shifting Kieran in his arms and dashing forward. "Come on!"

Sammy, Agatha, and Greta followed close behind. I brought up the rear.

"Close it up!" I shouted. "So they can't see where we've gone."

Sammy paused and turned back, tapping at the screen. Behind me, the first wall of hedges jerked back and forth in their tracks, straining to close like a pair of broken elevator doors. "It's not working. Run! Fast!" He took off again, and everyone followed.

Except for me.

I'd run out of hose.

Greta turned back halfway. "What are you waiting for?"

"I'm covering our retreat!" I sprayed some water on a new spot that blazed up on my left.

"Don't be stupid!" Greta yelled. "Come on!"

But before I could drop the hose, the nozzle was yanked out of my hand.

A Bend Sinister agent was standing at the foot of the hill. He dragged my hose away and casually raised his Tesla rifle.

I crouched down, barely ten feet away, an easy target. I had no weapon, no way to dodge or deflect the bolt.

But he wasn't looking at me at all. He was aiming over my head. At Greta.

And behind him stood my dad, his arms crossed, watching as his flunky prepared to kill my friend.

It came down to this. I'd lured my dad here, stupidly tried to outsmart him, and because of that, the girl who'd become my best friend was going to get killed. I'd been trying to think like one of the Guard, but *I'd* done this. So I had to undo it.

As the agent squeezed the trigger, I didn't think.

I jumped straight up, right into the path of the bolt.

Okay, so I was probably going to die. Somewhere deep down I knew that, but weirdly, the thought didn't bother me all that much. The fear that I might fail to save Greta was worse. *Protect Greta*, I'd been told. *That's what a Blood Guard does.*

I am Blood Guard. So that's what I did.

I leaped high, my arms and legs spread-eagled so that I made as big a shield as possible. The Tesla bolt crackled. And at that moment, the maze mechanism gave way, the hedges that had been stuck open like elevator doors whooshing shut.

And I came down on the tiled pathway.

I'd shut my eyes tight at the last second, because even though I was willing to die to save Greta, I wasn't really so keen to watch it happen. Weirdly, I felt no pain—because of the shock, I guess. I was cold and wet, covered in my own blood, no doubt.

I finally opened my eyes to find myself lying in an ankle-deep puddle of dirty water. From my hose. In front of me, the hedges flickered and burned. They'd caught the bolt. I wasn't hurt at all.

"I'm alive!" I laughed.

"Come *on*!" Greta shouted from up ahead. So I got up and sloshed after her.

I heard the broken hedgerow behind me ratchet open again and chanced a look back.

My dad was watching me and Greta with his chin in his hand. Almost like he was studying us.

The hedges closed again and he was gone. The next time they opened, the female Hand was standing next to my dad. Her hands were by her sides but glowing, and as she raised them and drew them together, fire ignited anew in the hedges on both sides of us, burning *inward* toward the center of our pathway—the flames didn't rise up like normal, but jetted sideways, fingers of fire that chased after us from hedge to hedge. Right away, I could feel the heat.

Worse, I could see the tongues of flame reaching for Greta.

I ran as hard as I could, my feet splashing in the dirty water on the tiled pathway, and at the last moment dove forward onto my belly.

It wasn't Dawkins or my mom who'd trained me to do that; it was my dad.

He was the one who bought me the Slip 'N Slide when I was six, and he was the one who used it with me until it fell apart.

I shot across the tile right into Greta's legs.

"*Ugh!*" she shouted, splashing in the dirty water. But then she saw the flames knitting themselves together above us, in the space where she'd been just a moment before. "Um, thanks."

"Stay low," I said.

So on elbows and knees, we crawled, grateful for the steel planters that kept the horizontal fire from spreading all the way down to the ground.

All of a sudden the mechanism beneath us engaged again, and one wall after another moved into place behind us, blocking us from the Hand and her magic. We stood up and walked forward, out of the dead maze and onto the living grass.

All of our friends except for Dawkins were twenty-five yards away, crouched around Kieran. When they saw us emerge, Sammy looked up from the iPad, smiled, and waved.

Ogabe ran over. "I'd worried we'd lost you." He pulled me and Greta into one giant hug with his enormous arms. "Thank God you two are safe."

Safe? In my mind's eye, all I could see was my dad, watching the two of us.

He knows, I thought. *He knows about Greta.*

CHAPTER 24
PEOPLE IN GLASS HOUSES

The entire hedge maze was burning now, an enormous ring of fire five hundred feet across that darkened the afternoon sky with black smoke. The only way to stop Bend Sinister agents, I knew, was to kill their Hand or burn them. Maybe this would do the trick. *No one will be able to come out of that alive*, I thought. *Not even dad.*

I felt a wave of guilt. Should I be happy if my dad were killed? Sad? I didn't know how to think about it. All I knew was that no normal person would be able to escape that fire.

And then someone *did*, chopping his way out through a burning hedge wall.

The figure staggered away from the maze, saber in hand. His hair and clothes were aflame, but that didn't stop him from waving at us before dropping to the ground and rolling.

Ogabe galloped over to him.

"Is that . . . Jack?" Agatha said.

"I know it's hard to believe," Greta told her, "but he'll be okay."

I crossed my fingers, more from habit than anything. I still wasn't quite sure how Dawkins' regenerative powers worked, but like Greta, I had faith.

"Guys, someone else is coming," Sammy said, looking the other way.

The four of us watched as a white van turned off the main drive and gunned across the grass toward the hedge maze.

"Good guys or bad guys?" Agatha asked.

"The cavalry come at last," Dawkins said, walking up with Ogabe. He was bare-chested and bare-headed, his hair all singed off, the skin looking new and bright pink. Even as he spoke, I could see a shimmery fuzz of blond hair growing back across his skull.

The van bounced across the flagstone paths and pulled to a stop. Greta's dad climbed out of the driver's side. "Smoke signals, Jack?"

Dawkins spread his arms wide. "I had to find some way to get your attention, Gaspar."

The passenger's side door popped open and my mother burst out. She barely slowed down before slamming into me and hugging me up off the ground.

"Mom!" I said. "Take it easy!"

"Be quiet, Evelyn," she said, crushing me hard. "Just be quiet."

I shut up and hugged her back. It felt good.

"It was supposed to be a risk-free mission," my mom said into my hair. "Safe. Easy. Not . . . whatever it turned out to be."

"We're okay," I said. "Except, um . . . Dad's here."

"What?" My mom gripped my shoulders. "Where?"

"In there." We looked back at the burning maze. "No way he got out of that, right?"

"We should assume the Bend Sinister Head escaped," Dawkins said. "His agents would no doubt sacrifice themselves to save their leader."

"But he may now be without the protection of a Hand and its agents," Ogabe said.

The three of them stopped and looked at me. And I knew why: No matter how awful the Bend Sinister Head was, no matter what he'd done, he was always going to be my dad. They were looking at me to take the lead.

"This is our chance," I said. "We should get him." I was afraid to tell them what I was really thinking, which was *Hurry—he knows about Greta.*

"Absolutely." Dawkins clapped me on the back. "What Ronan said. We should move, and move quickly, before the Head joins forces with another Hand who is on the premises. Bree, you and Ronan come with me, Agatha, and Ogabe. Gaspar, stay by the van with this unconscious boy, the other kids, and the Four Horsemen. Just in case things go poorly at the house."

"I want to go with you and Ronan," Greta said.

"You don't get a vote in this," Mr. Sustermann said. "And no arguments."

"Who's Agatha?" My mom raised an eyebrow. "And the Four Horsemen?"

"The Dobermans," Dawkins said. "They are very smart and reliably brave. As for Agatha—"

"That's me," Agatha said, adding, "I'm not actually a kid."

"It's a long story," Dawkins said, "but Agatha knows that house better than anyone. She is coming with us."

"Why's this place got to be so big?" Dawkins complained. "Fifteen minutes just to cross a lawn!"

Sitting by itself on that wide field of grass, the house looked like something out of a horror movie. It seemed to get darker as we got closer. The other Blood Guard van was parked out front, as well as two black SUVs.

"The other four with us went directly to the house," my mom said. "If there's another Hand there, they've probably engaged him."

"This other Hand is dangerous," Dawkins said. "He can disable his opponents by stealing their senses, leave them with no control of their bodies."

As we ran, I said to Dawkins, "There's more. My dad, I think he knows."

"Knows *what* precisely, Ronan?" Dawkins huffed.

"Greta," I whispered. "I tried to save her and he was watching and . . . he knows. I'm sure of it."

Dawkins exhaled loudly. "Team," he said, as he ran beside me, "our objectives in that house are threefold. Foremost, we urgently need to apprehend the Head. Ogabe, that's your mission. Do whatever you can to stop him from leaving this estate.

"Second, we need to protect our own from that Hand and, if possible, apprehend him. Bree, I'll leave that to you." We'd reached the drive in front of the house, our feet loud on the gravel.

"Third," Dawkins said, huffing as we slowed down, "the Damascene 'Scope is functional."

"Functional?" my mom repeated. "As in, we can use it to restore Flavia's soul?"

"Theoretically. At any rate, the device needs securing. So Ronan and I will see to that."

"I'll help," Agatha said.

"A flea would be of more assistance," Dawkins said. "It's three times your weight!"

"I'm the only one here who has ever used it." I could almost hear the eye roll in Agatha's voice.

"Point taken," Dawkins said.

When we opened the door to the museum, all that greeted us was quiet. Dawkins signaled for my mom to go upstairs and Ogabe to go downstairs, and then he, Agatha, and I eased into the museum and quietly shut the door behind us.

We found the mirror room just as we'd left it—the sliding door standing open, the purple tarp draped over

239

something in the center of the room, the mirrored walls glimmering with reflected light.

We'd taken only four steps into the room when I remembered that the tarp shouldn't be covering anything at all. Dawkins and I had hidden under it with Agatha, but then we'd left.

I tugged the tarp aside. Beneath it were the bodies of two of the Blood Guard. We didn't need to confirm that the men were dead; living people don't fold themselves up like that.

Dawkins swiftly drew his sword as voices drifted in from the greenhouse.

"If it won't unscrew, we'll just have to take it with the tripod still attached."

Patch Steiner, from the other side of the center mirrored panel.

Dawkins pointed at me and Agatha and then pointed back to the museum. His meaning was clear: *Get to safety and get help.*

And then Steiner's voice fell silent. We heard an enormous *sniff.*

"Something smells suspiciously like burnt hair and flesh—is that you, Mr. Dawkins? Did you survive that nasty fire?" Steiner laughed. "I am so glad you chose to approach through the mirror room."

In front of me, Dawkins slumped, his hand with the sword relaxing so that the weapon clanked to the floor, his jaw going slack.

"Good, I have your attention. Just stand there a moment while I take care of this. Your gun, Number Three. Fire it at that mirrored divider there."

I grabbed Dawkins' hand and yanked him and Agatha to the ground as the room erupted in purple lightning.

The air over our heads sizzled with electricity, the beam ricocheting between the mirrored panels. Steiner's Number Three didn't release the trigger, just kept firing away, until with a shriek of anger, Agatha took Dawkins' sword from his limp hand and scrambled around the corner.

A man howled in pain, the lightning disappeared, and Agatha screamed.

Steiner must have been distracted, because suddenly Dawkins was back in control of his body. In one motion, he was up and running after her.

CHAPTER 25

LIGHTNING ON A BOTTLE

I crawled around the corner on hands and knees, wondering whether I'd be able to help anyone at all.

Within the greenhouse, Patch Steiner stood dead center behind the Damascene 'Scope. Two of his agents, a man and a woman, were standing near the 'Scope, tools in their hands, clearly in the process of trying to remove it from the tripod. A third man was on the ground just inside the door, stuck through the middle with Dawkins' sword, struggling to reach his Tesla rifle.

And in a tiny heap in front of the 'Scope: Agatha.

Dawkins narrowed the odds right away. He charged the nearest agent, knocking the man's sword aside and shoving him into the floor-to-ceiling glass pane behind him.

It shattered, and the agent sailed through and onto the lawn. Before the man even landed, Dawkins crouched, ducking a chop of the woman's cutlass, then leaped up, knocking his head into her chin.

She staggered and started to slide to the floor, but Dawkins grabbed her legs and swung her up and around in big circles, like an enormous, well-dressed human sledgehammer.

A Blood Guard finds weapons in whatever he has at hand. Even if that weapon is a Bend Sinister agent.

Dawkins laughed. "I don't need to be able to see to get you, Steiner." With each swing of the body, he took a step forward while Steiner backed out of range.

No one noticed as I crawled over to Agatha. I shook her thin shoulder, but she didn't respond.

That's when I saw it: under the 'Scope, next to the massive wooden tripod, was an open aluminum case. A stenciled tag on the lid read EVANGELINE BIRK, but I didn't care about that, because tucked within was a familiar silvered flask, a bottle about as big as a thermos. It was frosty with condensation, and curls of cool mist rose from it.

The Conceptacle.

Here. Just lying out in the open like it was part of someone's lunchbox.

So my dad had taken the bait, after all, and had brought the Pure's soul here in the hopes of destroying it.

I inched across the floor as quietly as possible, until I could grasp the Conceptacle. It took some work to pry it out of the foam packing, but it finally came loose with a jerk.

I almost dropped it. The bottle was heavy—a lot heavier than I expected—and so cold to the touch that I could feel the moisture on my palm immediately freezing. I tried to let it go, but it was no use: my hand might as well have been welded to it.

I looked up and saw Dawkins still spinning like an Olympic hammer thrower, faster and faster, the unconscious Bend Sinister's body whirring past with each revolution, her hair a dark fan atop her head.

"Stop that!" Patch Steiner yelled, his head tipped back at the ceiling.

"Sure thing," Dawkins said. "I was just waiting for you to speak up!"

He let go and the agent's body flew across the room—barely missing Steiner as the fat man lurched to the right.

"Appalling how you used my poor Ms. Three," Steiner said, clucking his tongue.

"Appalling that I *missed*," Dawkins said, blinking. "Whose eyes are you using now? That goon with the gun?"

I'd forgotten that Bend Sinister agents were unkillable; only by destroying their Hand could they be stopped. And I hadn't noticed as the agent Agatha had attacked got back to his feet. He staggered over next to Steiner and aimed his rifle at Dawkins.

"I'm told you can't be killed," Steiner said. "I am certainly willing to put that to the test." He swept out his left hand to point at Agatha. "She died easily enough."

That was when he—or I guess the borrowed eyes of his agent—spotted me.

"Where did you come from?" he snapped.

"I have the Pure's soul!" I said, raising the Conceptacle. If I could distract Steiner long enough, maybe Dawkins could get the upper hand.

"Put that down!" Steiner told me as the agent brought the muzzle of his rifle toward me. "Or . . ."

I couldn't have dropped it if I tried; my hand was frozen to it like a tongue to a flagpole in winter. Not that Steiner needed to know that. "Or what?" I asked, slowly crawling backward.

"Or we will do what we should have done the first time: shoot you."

Dawkins hooked the toe of his left foot under the hilt of the discarded sword on the floor.

"Now, Mr. Dawkins," Steiner said, wagging a finger. "You know as well as I that you will not be able to bring that sword up in time to stop the bolt from that gun. You don't move faster than the speed of light. Of course, I could always immobilize you instead."

"But you can only take on one person at a time, can't you?" Dawkins smiled. "Ronan, throw the Conceptacle."

"To you?" I asked.

"No!" Dawkins said. "At *him*."

"Do not throw it!" Steiner bellowed as the man swung the gun back toward Dawkins. "The Conceptacle is glass and can break, you know. That's why it is carried in that padded case."

"Better it break and that soul be released than that these brutes destroy it," Dawkins said.

"If you want me to spare your friend Dawkins," Steiner said, "you will replace it where you found it."

I flexed my fingers. The bottle stayed snug in my palm. "No. It's mine now. I think I'm going to keep it."

Steiner waved his palm at me. "Shoot the boy."

Dawkins kicked the sword up into his hand and lunged forward at the same moment the agent snapped the rifle my way and squeezed the trigger.

And then Steiner took my eyesight.

I don't know if he did it because he didn't want me to be able to see what was coming my way, or because he wanted to witness my death firsthand. All I know is that a curtain of nothing dropped down on my brain at the moment his flunky fired off the Tesla bolt.

As my last act, I threw the Conceptacle away from myself as hard as I could, straight at where I thought Steiner's head had been.

But of course it didn't go anywhere, because it was stuck to my palm.

When the jaggedy bolt of lightning from the Tesla rifle reached me, my arm was fully extended in front of me, my fingers wide, the Conceptacle painfully glued in place.

The beam struck the curved, mirrored surface of the bottle dead-on.

Dawkins' sword must have connected, because Steiner gasped and my vision snapped back into place with a jolt.

The bolt reflected off the Conceptacle in a bright, crackling arc—tearing across Dawkins' arm and through the leaded windowpanes of the greenhouse.

But I was still falling forward, holding the bottle out in front of me. As the bolt crawled along the curved side of the Conceptacle, the angle of reflection narrowed, and the beam ricocheted back at the shooter.

But it hit Patch Steiner first.

The lightning caught him in the center of his chest. His white suit blackened and caught fire, but he no longer seemed to notice or care: his entire body began convulsing, and he fell to his knees and forward onto his face at the same moment the gun's discharge cut off.

"Destroy a Hand, destroy the agents he controls," Dawkins said, resting the point of his cutlass against Steiner's head. But the only movement from Steiner was the crackle of flames from his suit.

"Is he dead?" I asked.

He nodded. "That was some kind of brilliant what you did with that mirrored bottle, Ronan."

I snapped my hand up and down in the air. "It's stuck."

But Dawkins was already ignoring me. He'd sheathed his sword and gone to Agatha.

He sank to his knees and pulled her into his lap. Cradling her, he said, "Come on, Aggie. I only just got you back, you can't go now. Not again. Not yet."

She stirred. Then she opened her eyes and tried to sit up. "That smarts," she said.

"Oh, come now," Dawkins said, a small smile on his face. "A bit of pain never hurt no one."

"That makes absolutely no sense, Jack," she said, wheezing. "Ooh, laughing hurts—I think I've broken some ribs."

"I promise to make no more jokes until you're better," he said.

"Are they all dead?" Agatha looked around the greenhouse, then noticed me behind Dawkins. "Ronan. Why are you carrying that bottle?"

"It's a Pure's soul. We got it back from Patch Steiner." I held up my hand. "It's frozen to my skin."

"Ha—ouch." Agatha said, chuckling and wincing.

"Ronan," Dawkins said, standing and cradling Agatha against his chest. "Let's find a safe place to wait for your mum and Ogabe. We've already lost enough in this fight. Until we hear that your dad is captured or run away, I'd rather not risk losing anything else."

"You're right," I said, raising my hand. "We have Flavia's soul." Whatever else had happened, this, at least, we could fix. "It's time she got it back."

CHAPTER 26
OUR FINAL EXAM

We gathered in the dining room and studied the Gauntlet, which was still in pieces in the center of the oily rag Greta had tied it up in.

"It's quite a beautiful thing, isn't it?" my mom said.

"Beautiful but deadly," Agatha said. "After Flavia's procedure, we should destroy it."

Just then a team of Brazilian Blood Guard, led by a man named Bartolomeu with a huge bushy moustache, arrived with Flavia. They wheeled her into the mirror room and spent the afternoon preparing her. Agatha supervised, doing what she called "the fine calibrations," making sure that Flavia's heart was located in the exact point where the reflected beams converged.

Meanwhile, Ogabe, my mom, and Mr. Sustermann prepared the Damascene 'Scope. They placed their Verity Glasses into the device, opened the crystal-walled portal where the soul would be deposited, and waited for Agatha to say everything was ready to go.

While everyone else got things set up, Dawkins and I waited in the museum.

I massaged the bandage across my palm where the Conceptacle had frozen. Dawkins and my mom had freed me by running warm water over my hand and the bottle, but there was a narrow area that had been stuck fast, and with a quick "Sorry 'bout this, Ronan!" Dawkins had yanked it free.

It had ripped a long strip of flesh right out of my hand. It hurt so much that I didn't say anything at all, just blinked away tears while my mom washed away the blood, covered the wound in ointment, and wrapped my hand in gauze.

"That may scar, honey," my mom said, frowning.

I looked at the Conceptacle. A finger-wide band of my frosty skin was stuck fast to it.

"A scar might be kind of cool," I said, the pain already dulling under the tight dressing. "Might make me look a little dangerous."

"Scars are not 'cool,' Ronan," my mom said. "They're reminders of pain."

I thought about how close I'd come to getting killed—how close we'd *all* come—and said, "I want a reminder. So that I never forget any of this."

Now I tried flexing my hand and got a twinge of pain. No way I could have worn the Glass Gauntlet, even if I'd wanted to. "Are you sure Agatha's the right person to do this?" I asked.

"I am absolutely *not* sure," Dawkins said, leaning over to peer into a display case. "Because Agatha, my Aggie, is also the woman who became Agatha Glass, who even she admits was evil personified. Are they one and the same? Do we give her a pass for having killed people, for plotting to steal the body of one of our friends? It seems wrong somehow."

"But it wasn't her fault," I said. "The Blood Guard did that to her."

He straightened up and looked at me. "Please: they were a bunch of Blood Guard *outcasts* . . . who later helped usher the Bend Sinister into the modern age."

"Members of the Guard joined the Bend Sinister?" I said. "But . . . they're not alike. We're the good guys and they're . . ."

"Evil? Yes, but for some people, those qualities are two sides of a coin." He looked down at his hands. "Whatever the case, their wonky mechanism killed all the good in Agatha. And their Glass Gauntlet literally killed my friend Spinks."

"Sorry," I said, because I couldn't think of what else to say.

He shrugged. "Oh, Spinks has been dead for ages, of course. I'm just sad to know he went in such a horrible way, and at the hands of people I'd sent to help."

"But you're going to let Agatha use the Glass Gauntlet now?"

"She volunteered," Dawkins said, shrugging. "She's the only one who has ever seen the Gauntlet in action, she's the right physical age to use the device, and frankly, I am not about to let you, or Sammy, or"—he grimaced—"Greta try the thing on for size. She'd never let us forget it! Speaking of which, I really ought to go help Agatha prepare. I'll come find you when it's time."

Greta, Sammy, and I anxiously waited on the back lawn, watching the sunset and glancing at the greenhouse every now and then. There wasn't anything for us to do, but Dawkins told us to stay close, so we kept ourselves busy throwing a ball for the dogs. They fell all over each other chasing it down and then practically tackled us every time they brought it back. It was as if no one had ever played with them before.

It all might have been fun if I hadn't been obsessing about Flavia in the mirror room, wondering whether Agatha would be able to restore her soul, or whether we were too late. I watched as Greta wound up and shot the ball like a major-league pitcher.

"Nice throw," I said.

"I was an MVP in my Little League," she said.

"Why does that not surprise me?" Sammy looked back at the house. "What do you think they're going to do with Kieran?"

Kieran had finally woken up that morning, but he didn't have much to say. He was like someone who'd suffered a long sickness—kind of fuzzy on the details about exactly what had happened to him. "Did I win?" he mumbled.

"Sure," Greta had told him. "You totally won."

"Good," he'd murmured, and then he fell right back to sleep.

"Depends on how much he remembers," I said now, taking the slobbery ball from Pestilence—or maybe it was Famine—I couldn't keep them straight. I tossed the ball in the direction of the garage and watched the Four Horsemen tear after it.

Dawkins leaned out the broken window of the greenhouse and shouted, "Greta, Ronan, Sammy—we're ready."

So we left the dogs and jogged over to watch Agatha reverse the horrible thing my father had done.

It was crowded in the greenhouse. In addition to the three of us, there were Dawkins, Ogabe, my mom, Mr. Sustermann, and Agatha. The Conceptacle was sitting on a wooden chair, curls of vapor rising from it.

"Here goes," Agatha said, sliding the glassy thumb part of the Gauntlet over her hand. Next was the palm and first two fingers, then the ring finger and pinky part of the glove. The pieces snapped together with a loud click, the seams disappearing where the glass edges met. She snapped the back of the hand into place, and a red glow kindled deep within in the glass.

She sucked in a sharp breath. "This hurts."

"Sorry, Aggie," Dawkins said, and he lifted up the final piece of the Gauntlet, the brass band that cuffed the wrist. He locked it into place around the base of the glove, and suddenly the Gauntlet was blazing bright red.

253

"How do I uncap the Conceptacle?" Dawkins asked.

Gritting her teeth, Agatha said, "You don't. Everyone stand back." She opened her red right hand wide, and beams of bright light shot forth from the thumb and each finger.

The silvered glass of the Conceptacle seemed to eddy away from the red light's reflection. Then Agatha closed her hand around it.

The silver rippled away from her fingers, leaving the glass clear where she touched it and allowing a white glow to burn through—a glow brighter even than the fingers of light Agatha manipulated.

Agatha closed her fist around the ball of light and the Conceptacle shattered. "I've got it!" she gasped. She turned her head away and blinked. Then she slowly walked to the Damascene 'Scope, pressing her fist against the crystal chamber inside, and opened the Glass Gauntlet again.

It was like she'd dropped a little piece of the sun into the 'Scope. I had to turn away, but I could still feel the heat against my face.

"It's in, it's in," Agatha said, sagging backward. "Close the housing."

Ogabe reached over and turned something on the 'Scope, and the wide brass skin of the cylinder rotated and covered the crystal chamber.

Suddenly the light in the room was normal again.

"I think I'm sunburned," Greta whispered, gingerly touching her cheeks.

"I'm going to open the shutter now," Agatha said.

The seven of us edged against the glass walls of the greenhouse as Agatha reached up with her left hand, turned a knob, and pulled a lever.

After the blinding brightness of the grasped soul, the flash of light when the soul was beamed into the mirror room was almost a disappointment. A flash of heat and light, and then Agatha raised the lever again, turned a couple of knobs, and kneeled down on the tile of the greenhouse.

"That does it," she said, resting her gauntleted right hand on the ground. "Please, somebody, get this thing off of me."

There wasn't much of an obvious change in Flavia. She was still in her coma, still thin and wasted-looking. But now, when we looked at her through our Verity Glasses, her soul burned bright in her body. My mom slipped off the locket she'd worn all summer and placed it back around Flavia's neck, saying, "We mothers need to stick together." Bartolomeu smiled under his bushy moustache and thanked us, and then he and his team took Flavia away. I couldn't imagine how they'd hide her from the Bend Sinister or what they'd tell her when she woke up, but that was a problem for her team now.

It was Greta I needed to worry about.

My dad had escaped. The grounds had been thoroughly searched, but we couldn't find any trace of him. It was like he'd never been there at all.

"Maybe he's dead," I said to my mom after Flavia was gone, while she, Dawkins, and I packed up the things in the greenhouse. It would be easier that way—if my dad had perished in the hedge maze. I wouldn't have to think about him anymore, wouldn't have to worry about the terrible things he'd do to Greta if he got his hands on her. "Dawkins barely got out of that fire. It could have killed Dad, too."

"There were only six bodies, Ronan," she said. "The Hand and her agents."

A paranoid part of me was sure he was hanging around, waiting to kill Greta at the first opportunity he had, but Dawkins insisted he was long gone.

"The thing about your dad," he said, "is he's a Head—he's not a fighter, he's a plotter. The last thing he wants is to meet one of us without a bunch of Hands and agents around him."

"A coward, you mean," I said, but Dawkins shook his head.

"Cowardice doesn't come into it. He's part of the brains of the operation, right? He has a duty to preserve himself, so that he can direct others to die for him another day." Dawkins pointed to the tag stenciled on the Conceptacle's case. "You see that name there?"

"Who is Evangeline Birk?" I asked, reading it.

"The supreme boss of the Bend Sinister," my mom said. "She was rumored to have died decades ago."

"But if there's a case marked for transport to her," Dawkins said, "then it is likely she is alive."

"What's that got to do with my dad?" I asked.

"He was bringing that to her before you cleverly diverted him here," Dawkins said. Despite myself, I felt a flicker of pride at having done that. "Now he'll be desperate to offer his boss something in return for the Pure soul he's lost."

"Greta." I felt weak. He was going to come after her with everything he had. "What are we going to do?"

"Well, first, we have to protect Greta's mother before the Bend Sinister locates her," my mom said.

"Second," Dawkins said, "as we know the Bend Sinister will be coming for her, we need to assemble in force to capture them."

"And third," my mom said, dusting off her hands, "we need to let Greta think this is entirely her idea."

"How are we going to do that?" I asked.

"Greta's been begging for a homecoming all summer." Dawkins' old grin appeared. "So we're going to give it to her."

EPILOGUE

A PROMISE KEPT, WITH DOGS

I was happy, and I felt guilty about it.

So many terrible things had happened. Two of our fellow Blood Guard had been killed by Patch Steiner and the Bend Sinister. A whole bunch of us almost burned up along with the hedge maze. My dad had gotten away again—this time, with knowledge about Greta.

But the people I most cared about in the world were safe—at least for now—and we had undone some of my father's awful work. I couldn't help but feel happy about that.

And on top of all that, we were heading back to my hometown, Brooklyn.

Agatha, it turned out, owned a helicopter.

"The controls were adjusted to my size," she explained before takeoff. Using the Glass Gauntlet had left Agatha looking even paler than she'd been before, practically translucent. She looked so much like a sickly little kid that it had been strange to see her pull a flight helmet over her colorless hair and grab the joystick. "You'll all want to put on your helmets. This thing can be pretty loud."

"Just how loud is *loud*?" Greta asked, picking up one of the heavy military-looking helmets.

"Would you mind?" Agatha asked, handing back a cloth sack. "Sound-dampening headphones for the Dobermans."

So: pretty loud, then.

"I still don't understand why we're bringing the Dobermans." Sammy scratched his head.

"You don't for a moment think I'd leave the dogs behind, do you?" Dawkins asked. "Who would feed them in our absence? Who would tuck them into bed?"

Sammy laughed. "Dogs don't need tucking into bed."

"Shows how much *you* know," Dawkins replied.

The dogs didn't mind the headphones at all. In fact, they jostled each other to get fitted with a pair. Afterward, each flopped down in a curl of fur. Before the last lay down, he rolled a chewed-up red ball against Sammy's feet.

Sammy wiped it dry on his khakis. "There's no room to play ball in here, War," he said, his voice coming through speakers in my helmet.

"I think that's Pestilence, actually," Greta said. "He has that narrow stripe of black between his eyes. The one with the black paws is War."

"Cut the dumb chatter, you three," Dawkins said, catching Greta's eye. "If we are going to get you to Brooklyn in one piece, we'd better let Agatha focus on flying."

Below us, the trees and hills were cloaked in shadow, except where the twilight was cut through by cars' white headlights and red taillights flowing through the dark.

"Thanks, Ronan," Greta said. "For remembering your promise back in Wilson Peak."

I smiled at her. Sometimes keeping a promise is the easiest thing in the world.

"Why are you thanking *Ronan*?" Dawkins complained. "It was *me* who engineered this escape, not scar-hand Truelove back there."

I ran my thumb over the band of smooth pink skin on my palm. I was stupidly pleased about it.

"Besides, it is thanks to me that you three won't get into trouble."

Greta frowned. "My dad isn't going to like that I just disappeared."

"Sometimes it can be easier to ask forgiveness later, than to receive permission beforehand, Greta. This is one of those times. Besides, we have only a tiny head start on them. While we are gallivanting around Brooklyn, they'll be readying an assault on Evangeline Birk and the rest of the Bend Sinister." He glanced over and caught my eye and I knew he was thinking of the same thing I was: my dad.

"Brooklyn!" Sammy said, grinning. "I've never been to New York!" He pressed his face against the Plexiglas window of the cockpit. "Or in a helicopter. Or in a plane."

"Greta," Dawkins said at last, "I don't wish to alarm you, but I worry that the Bend Sinister may have identified

260

you as one of Ronan's friends. They can't get to Ronan, but they can get to those he loves—or, in this case, someone close to one of his dear friends."

"You think they'd go after my mom?" Greta asked, sitting forward.

Dawkins shrugged. "Who can say? It's a possibility. So we will move in fast, convince your mum to come with us, and then spirit her away to safety. Just until we've confirmed that there is no threat."

"Okay," Greta said, nodding.

"We are a more nimble team, one that has proven itself in the field"—he looked at each of us in turn—"for which I in particular am very grateful. The size of our team is ideal—it will be much easier for us to get in there fast and get out with her."

The helicopter would get us to New York quickly, I knew—Agatha thought we'd be there in a bit more than an hour—but would that be fast enough to beat my dad? He had a full day's head start, but he'd left the Glass estate by himself. It would take him a while to get reinforcements, wouldn't it? But would he even need them? Mrs. Sustermann knew him. If he got to her first, all he would have to do would be to walk up, ring Mrs. Sustermann's doorbell, and . . .

"We are going need a plan," I said. "A *good* plan, Jack."

"A flawless plan," Greta said.

So we came up with one.

ACKNOWLEDGMENTS

Thank you

Deborah Bass

Dan Bennett

Genevieve Herr

Ruth Katcher

Timony Korbar

Emily Lamm

Maggie Sivon

Stephanie Thwaites

Vivienne To

Above and beyond

Bruce Coville

Melanie Kroupa

Ted Malawer

Kelsey Skea

Beth Ziemacki

CARTER ROY worked some three-dozen jobs ranging from movie theater projectionist to delivery truck driver before finally ending up as an editor for a major publisher, where he edited hundreds of books before leaving to write. The author of *The Blood Guard*, he is also an award-winning short-story writer. He lives in New York City. Find out more at www.carterroybooks.com.